Maigret in
Holland

Georges Simenon

Maigret in Holland

Translated by Geoffrey Sainsbury

A Harvest Book
A Helen and Kurt Wolff Book
Harcourt Brace & Company
San Diego   New York   London

Requests for permission to make copies of any part of
the work should be mailed to: Permissions Department,
Harcourt Brace & Company,
6277 Sea Harbor Drive, Orlando, Florida 32887-6777.

This is a translation of *Un Crime en Hollande*.

Maigret is a registered trademark of the
Estate of Georges Simenon.

Library of Congress Cataloging-in-Publication Data
Simenon, Georges, 1903–1989
[Crime en Hollande. English]
Maigret in Holland/Georges Simenon; translated
by Geoffrey Sainsbury. — 2nd ed.
p. cm.
ISBN 0-15-155159-6
ISBN 0-15-600084-9
"A Helen and Kurt Wolff Book."
I. Title.
PQ2637.I53C713   1993
843'.912 — dc20   92-30504

Printed in the United States of America
First Harvest edition 1994
B C D E

Maigret in
Holland

– 1 –

A Pedigree Calf

Maigret had only a faint idea of what it was all about when he arrived one May afternoon in Delfzijl, a small town squatting on the low coast in the extreme north-east of the Netherlands.

A certain Jean Duclos, a professor at the University of Nancy, had been on a lecture tour through the countries of northern Europe. At Delfzijl he had been the guest of Monsieur Popinga, who was a teacher on the training ship there, and this Monsieur Popinga had been murdered. Though the French professor could hardly have been called a suspect, he had nevertheless been requested not to leave the town, and to hold himself at the disposal of the police.

That was about all Maigret knew, except for a rather confused report Jean Duclos had forwarded to the Paris police himself. He had at once informed the University of Nancy, whose authorities had then asked for a member of the Police Judiciaire to be sent to the spot.

It was just the job for Maigret, being semiofficial.

He had made it all the less formal by having taken no steps to warn the Dutch police that he was coming.

At the end of Jean Duclos's report was a list of the principal people involved, and it was this list that Maigret had been studying during the last half hour of his journey:

CONRAD POPINGA, the victim, forty-two, formerly a captain in the merchant service, now teaching cadets on the training ship at Delfzijl. Married. No children. Spoke English and German fluently, and fairly good French.

LIESBETH POPINGA, his wife. Daughter of the headmaster of a lycée in Amsterdam, a woman of considerable culture, including a thorough knowledge of French.

ANY VAN ELST, the latter's younger sister, on a visit of some weeks in Delfzijl, recently completed her degree in law. Twenty-five years old. Understands a good deal of French, but speaks it badly.

THE WIENANDS, living next door. Carl W. teaches mathematics on the training ship. Wife and two children. No French.

BEETJE LIEWENS, eighteen, daughter of a farmer who breeds pedigree cows. Has twice been to Paris. French quite good.

The names conveyed nothing to Maigret. He had been traveling for a night and half a day and wasn't feeling particularly enthusiastic.

Right from the start, he found Delfzijl disconcerting. At dawn he had found himself rolling through the traditional Holland of tulips. Then came Amsterdam,

2

which he already knew. But Drenthe, an endless stretch of heather, had taken him by surprise. A twenty-mile horizon sectioned by canals.

And what he now came to was something that bore no relation to the ordinary picture postcard of Holland. It was far more Nordic than anything he had imagined.

A small town. At the most, ten or fifteen streets paved with beautiful red tiles, as regularly laid as those of a kitchen floor. Low houses of brick, ornamented with a profusion of carved woodwork painted in cheerful colors.

The whole place was like a toy, all the more so because it was completely encircled by a dike. In this dike were openings with heavy lock gates, which were no doubt closed during spring tides.

Beyond was the estuary of the Ems River, and then the North Sea, a long silver ribbon of water. Ships were unloading their cargoes under the cranes on the quay. In the canals were innumerable sailing boats, big as barges and as heavy, built to withstand the open seas.

The sun shone brightly. The stationmaster was wearing a bright orange cap, to which he automatically raised his hand to salute the unknown passenger.

There was a café opposite. Maigret went in. But he hardly dared sit down. Not only was it scrubbed and polished like the most respectable of dining rooms, but also the atmosphere was equally homelike.

There was only one table, on which lay all the morning papers, fixed to wire frames. The proprietor, who was having a glass of beer with two customers, came over to welcome the newcomer.

"Do you speak French?" asked Maigret.

The proprietor shook his head, with a touch of embarrassment.

"Donnez-moi de la bière. . . . Bier!"

Having sat down, he once more scanned Professor Duclos's list. Somehow the last name seemed to him the most hopeful. He showed it to the proprietor, and two or three times pronounced the name:

"Liewens."

The three men began talking together. Then one of them stood up, a huge fellow wearing a fisherman's cap, who beckoned Maigret to follow. The inspector had not yet provided himself with Dutch money. When he offered a hundred-franc note, the proprietor waved it aside.

"Morgen! . . . Morgen!"

Tomorrow! So he'd have to come back! . . .

Yes, the atmosphere was certainly one of intimacy; it was all so simple and candid. Without a word, Maigret's guide led him through the streets of the little town. On the left, a large shed was full of old anchors, rope, lengths of cable, buoys, compasses. Gear was even spread out along the street. Farther on, a sailmaker was working on his doorstep. A confectioner's window exhibited a great choice of chocolates and complicated sweetmeats.

"Speak English?"

Maigret shook his head.

"Deutsch?"

Maigret shook his head again, at which the man relapsed into silence.

At the end of the street, open country began: green

meadows; a canal, most of whose surface was broken by floating tree trunks from northern countries waiting to be towed to their various destinations inland.

In the distance, a long roof of glazed tiles.

"Liewens!" said the man, pointing to it. *"Dag, mijnheer!"*

Maigret went on alone after doing his best to thank his guide, who had come nearly a quarter of an hour's walk to do a perfect stranger a good turn.

The sky was clear, the air extraordinarily limpid. The inspector skirted a lumberyard in which piles of oak, mahogany, and teak rose high as the houses.

There was a boat moored to the bank, children playing close by. Then nothing for more than half a mile but logs in the canal, white fences around fields where, here and there, magnificent cows were grazing. Then Liewens' farm.

And here was something else Maigret hadn't bargained for. The word "farm" had a different meaning here from the one he was accustomed to. For him the word had always implied a thatched roof, a manure heap, the clucking of hens and cackle of geese.

The one he now came to was a fine new building surrounded by a large garden full of blooming flowers. Everything was trim and peaceful. On the canal opposite the house, a graceful mahogany rowing dinghy. By the gate, a woman's bicycle, nickel-plated.

He looked in vain for a bell; he called, but got no answer. A dog began barking.

To the left of the house was a long building with regularly spaced windows, which, however, had no curtains. It could have been taken for a shed had it not been so spick and span, and so obviously painted with an eye to the effect of its color.

The sound of mooing came from within, and Maigret, walking around some flower beds, found himself looking through a wide-open door.

The building was in fact a cowshed, though clean as any house. Red tiles everywhere gave a warm glow and even a feeling of sumptuousness. Gutters provided drainage. An ingenious mechanism controlled the fodder in the mangers. A pulley at the back of each stall—whose use Maigret found out only later—held up the cows' tails during milking to prevent dirt from being flicked into the pail.

The light inside was dim. All the cows were out except for one lying on its side in the first stall.

A young girl came up and began speaking to him in Dutch.

"Mademoiselle Liewens?"

"Yes . . . Are you French?"

While she spoke she looked toward the cow. There was something a little ironical about her smile, which Maigret did not understand right away.

Another thing that clashed with his preconceived ideas was that Beetje Liewens wore black rubber boots more like riding boots.

She was wearing a green silk dress, though it was almost entirely concealed by a white smock like that of a hospital nurse.

A ruddy face, perhaps too ruddy. A healthy sunny smile, which lacked subtlety. Big china-blue eyes and red hair.

At first she seemed to have some difficulty finding her words in French, but she soon got into her stride.

6

"Did you want to speak to my father?"

"No. To you."

She nearly burst out laughing.

"I'm afraid you'll have to excuse me. . . . My father's gone to Groningen and he won't be back until evening. Our two men are at the canal, fetching a load of coal. And the maid's out shopping. . . . And *this* is the moment this wretched cow has chosen to have her calf. We weren't expecting it at all, or I'd never have been left alone."

She was leaning against a windlass, which she had ready in case it was needed to assist in the calf's delivery.

Outside, the sun was shining brightly, reflected by her boots, which glistened in the dim light as though varnished. She had plump pink hands, the nails of which were carefully manicured.

"It's about Conrad Popinga . . ." began Maigret.

But she frowned. The cow had painfully scrambled to its feet and then sunk to the ground again.

"Here we are! . . . Would you like to help me?"

She snatched up the rubber gloves lying ready.

Thus Maigret began his investigation by aiding a purebred Frisian calf to come into the world—or, rather, by acting as assistant to this capable girl, whose easy movements showed her well versed in this work of the farm.

Half an hour later he and Beetje were bending over a copper tap lathering their hands and arms right up to the elbow.

"I daresay this is the first time you've put your hand to that job."

"It is."

She was eighteen years old. At least that's what Duclos had said. When she took off her white smock, her silk dress outlined a rounded figure. Perhaps the sunshine was showing her off to advantage, but she certainly seemed the kind of girl to turn a man's head.

"Come in. We can talk over a cup of tea. The maid's back."

The living room was austere, a little somber, but elegant and comfortable. The glass of the small windowpanes was faintly tinted, another detail new to Maigret.

A bookcase full of numerous works on cattle-breeding, handbooks of veterinary surgery. On the walls, gold medals and certificates that had been won in international shows.

And among the books the latest works of Claudel, André Gide, and Valéry.

Beetje's smile was coquettish.

"Would you like to see my room?"

She watched him closely for the impression it made on him. There was no bed, in the ordinary sense of the word, but a divan covered with blue velvet. The walls were covered with toile de Jouy. Bookshelves with more books. A doll that had been bought in Paris, all frills and furbelows.

It could almost have been called a boudoir, though it was a little heavy, ponderous for that.

"Quite like Paris, isn't it?"

"Tell me what happened last week."

Beetje's face clouded, though not very much—not enough to give the impression that she took the event very seriously.

No, it certainly was not weighing on her mind. Otherwise she would hardly have shown her room so proudly.

"You'll have some tea, won't you?"

They sat opposite each other. Between them the teapot, covered by a cozy.

Beetje still had to grope for a word now and again. In fact, she did more than grope. She fetched a dictionary, and sometimes there were long pauses while she looked for the exact expression she wanted.

A boat with a large gray sail glided slowly by on the canal. There was hardly any wind, so she was being punted along, threading her way through the logs that partially blocked the waterway.

"You haven't yet been to the Popingas'?"

"I arrived only an hour ago, and so far my time has been devoted to cattle-breeding."

"Ah, yes. . . . Conrad was a charming man, really very charming. . . . He'd spent many years at sea, and been to every country. Soon after he got his master's license, he married. It was for his wife's sake that he gave up the sea and accepted a post on the training ship. Rather dull . . . At first he had a fair-size boat, but Madame Popinga was frightened of the water, and in the end he sold it. . . . Since then he's only had a little boat on the canal. . . . Did you see mine as you came? . . . His is practically identical. . . . In the evenings he used to give private lessons to some of his pupils. He worked very hard."

"What was he like?"

She didn't understand at once. Then she went and got a photograph. It showed a tall, round-faced man, with pale clear eyes and closely cropped hair. He looked the picture of good health and good nature.

"That's Conrad. You wouldn't think he was forty, would you? . . . His wife is older. Maybe forty-five . . . I suppose you'll be seeing her. She's entirely different. Quite a different outlook. . . . Of course, everybody's Protestant here, but Liesbeth Popinga belongs to the strictest sect of all. She's very conservative. . . ."

"An active woman?"

"Yes, very. She's head of anything that has to do with charity."

"You don't like her?"

"Of course I do. . . . But . . . It's difficult to explain. . . . Her father's a headmaster, while I'm only a farmer's daughter. Do you understand? . . . Still, she's always very sweet and kind."

"And now? . . . What happened?"

"We often have lectures here. It's only a little town, but all the same we like to keep in touch with what's going on. Last Thursday we had Professor Duclos, from Nancy. You know him, of course."

She was astonished when Maigret told her he didn't, for she had assumed the professor to be one of the lights of French civilization.

"A great lawyer. He specializes in criminology and criminal psychology. . . . He talked to us about criminal responsibility, *la responsabilité des criminels*. Is that right? Stop me if I make mistakes.

"Madame Popinga is president of that society, and the lecturers always stay at her house. Often she invites people there to meet them.

"She did so this time. Not a real party. Just a few

10

friends . . . There was Professor Duclos, Conrad Popinga and his wife, Wienand, with his wife and children, and me."

"What time was it?"

"Rather late. About ten o'clock.

"The Popingas' house is more than half a mile from here, and it's on the Amsterdiep too. . . . The Amsterdiep—that's the canal you can see from where you're sitting. . . . We had tea and cakes, and there was some brandy. Conrad turned on the radio. . . . Oh, I forgot! Any was there too, Madame Popinga's sister. She's a lawyer. . . . Conrad wanted to dance, and we rolled up the carpet. . . . The Wienands left early, on account of the children—the little one had started crying. They live next door. . . . Toward midnight Any said she was tired. Then I went and got my bicycle. Conrad did the same. He saw me home.

"My father was waiting for me here. . . .

"It wasn't till next morning that we heard about it. The news was all over Delfzijl. . . .

"I don't think it was my fault. . . . When Conrad reached home, he went to put his bicycle away in the shed behind the house. Someone fired a revolver, and he fell. He opened his mouth, but died before he could speak."

She dried a tear that looked strangely out of place on that smooth cheek, red as a ripe apple.

"Is that all?"

"Yes. Detectives came over from Groningen to help the local police. . . . They came to the conclusion that the shot had been fired from the house. . . . And it seems that the professor was seen coming downstairs

11

with a revolver in his hand . . . the same revolver that killed Conrad."

"Professor Jean Duclos?"

"Yes. That's why they wouldn't let him go."

"So at the moment of the crime there was nobody in the house except Madame Popinga, her sister, Any, and Professor Duclos?"

"*Ya!*"

"And during the evening there had been those three, plus the Wienands, you, and Conrad?"

"There was Cor. I forgot him."

"Cor?"

"It's short for Cornélius. He's a cadet on the training ship, and he used to get private lessons from Conrad."

"When did he leave?"

"At the same time we did—I mean Conrad and me. He hadn't brought his bicycle. We walked together for a while, then we jumped on our bicycles and left him. . . . Do you take sugar?"

The tea steamed in the cups. A car had just driven up opposite the three steps that led to the front door. A moment later a man entered the room. He was tall, broad-shouldered, graying, and had a somber face. There was something heavy about him, which accentuated his placidity.

It was the farmer, Liewens. He stood still, waiting for his daughter to introduce him to the visitor. When that was done, he shook Maigret's hand heartily, but said nothing.

"My father doesn't speak French."

She poured a cup of tea for him, which he sipped,

still standing. Meanwhile, she told him in Dutch about the calf that had been born.

She must also have told him about Maigret, for he looked at the latter with surprise not unmixed with irony. Then, after stiffly taking his leave, he strode off to the cowshed.

"Have they arrested Professor Duclos?" asked Maigret as soon as he had gone.

"No. He's at the Hotel Van Hasselt. All they've done is keep a policeman there."

"What have they done with the body?"

"They've taken it to Groningen. That's twenty miles away. A big town, with a university, where Duclos gave a lecture the day before . . . It's awful, isn't it? . . . We don't know what to make of it. . . ."

No doubt it *was* awful. But it was difficult to realize it, probably because of that limpid atmosphere, the comfortable room in which Maigret was sitting, the tea steaming in the cups. In fact, the whole place was the antithesis of awfulness. A little toy town laid gently down by the seashore.

Outside could be seen, rising above the red tile roofs, the funnel and bridge of a big merchantman, unloading cargo. And boats on the Ems gliding slowly down toward the sea.

"Did Conrad often see you home?"

"Whenever I went to his house . . . He and I were great friends."

"Wasn't Madame Popinga jealous?"

That was a chance shot, prompted by the fact that Maigret's eyes had fallen on Beetje's inviting bosom.

"Why?"

13

"I don't know. . . . Going off like that . . . at night . . ."

She laughed, showing a row of healthy teeth.

"It's quite common in Holland. Cor often saw me home too."

"And he wasn't in love with you?"

She didn't answer yes or no. She giggled. That was the word for it. A little giggle of self-satisfaction.

Her father passed the window carrying the calf as though it were a baby. He stood it on the grass of the meadow in the sun.

The creature swayed on its slender legs, almost fell to its knees, suddenly pranced four or five yards, then stood stock-still.

"Did Conrad ever kiss you?"

Another giggle, but this time she blushed slightly.

"Yes."

"And Cor?"

This time she was inclined to be evasive. She looked away, hesitated, but finally said:

"Yes. He did too. . . . Why do you ask?"

She had a strange look on her face. Did she expect Maigret to follow suit and kiss her too?

Her father called her. She opened the window, and they talked for a while in Dutch. When she drew her head in it was to say:

"Excuse me . . . I must go into town to get the mayor. It's about the calf's pedigree. He has to be a witness, and it's very important. . . . Are you going back to Delfzijl?"

They went out together. She took her nickel-plated bicycle by the handlebar and wheeled it along. She

14

walked with a slight swing of her hips, which were already broad as a woman's.

"What a lovely day to be outside. . . . Poor Conrad will never . . . The public swimming places open tomorrow. He used to swim every day. He could stay as long as an hour in the water. . . ."

Maigret walked by her side, staring at the ground.

−2−

The Cap in the Bathtub

Maigret was always more interested in people than in places, but this time he noticed certain precise details about the place that he found very useful afterward. If it wasn't luck that made him do this, it can only have been his flair.

From the Liewens's farm to the Popingas' was just about twelve hundred yards. Both houses were by the canal, and the shortest way from one to the other was by the towpath. This canal was little used since the much bigger Ems canal had been made, to join Delfzijl and Groningen.

This one, the Amsterdiep, winding, muddy, shaded by beautiful trees, was used now only for lumber and by some of the smaller boats.

Farms were scattered here and there. A shipwright's yard . . .

Leaving the Popingas' house for the Liewens's, you would come first to the Wienands' place, which was only thirty yards away. Then a house that was being built.

Then a large piece of wasteland, and after that the lumberyard with its piles of cut logs.

Beyond was a bend in the canal, and then came another empty space. From there you could distinctly see the windows of the Popingas' house and, a little to the left, the white lighthouse over on the other side of town.

Maigret looked up at the lighthouse and asked: "Does the light shine this way?"

"Yes, when it comes around. It's a revolving light."

"So at night it lights up this part of the towpath?"

"Yes," she said again, with a little laugh, as though reminded of something that tickled her.

"Given away many a courting couple, I daresay!" grunted Maigret.

She left him just before they reached the Popingas' on the pretext of taking a shortcut, but really so as not to be seen with him.

Maigret did not stop. It was a modern brick house with a little garden in front and a vegetable garden behind. A path on the right-hand side, and on the left a patch of unused ground.

He preferred to go back to town, which was only five hundred yards away. Coming to the lock that separated the canal from the harbor, he stopped. The latter was alive with boats, ranging from one to three hundred tons, many made fast alongside each other.

To the left the Hotel Van Hasselt. He went in.

A large dark room with varnished paneling in which floated a complex smell of beer, schnapps, and floor

17

polish. A full-sized billiard table. A brass-railed table covered with newspapers.

As soon as Maigret entered, a man rose to his feet and came forward from his corner.

"Are you the person who has been sent by the French police?"

He was tall, thin, and bony, with a long face and strong features, horn-rimmed glasses, and thick hair standing up *en brosse.*

"You must be Professor Duclos?" answered Maigret.

He had not pictured him so young. Duclos might have been between thirty-five and thirty-eight, hardly more. But something about him struck Maigret as odd.

"You come from Nancy, I think?"

"To be accurate, I have a professorship there. Sociology . . ."

"But you weren't born in France?"

They were already sparring.

"In Switzerland, the French part. I'm now a naturalized French subject. I took my degrees in Paris and Montpellier."

"And you're a Protestant?"

"What makes you think so?"

It was difficult to say. Somehow or other it was written all over the man. Duclos belonged to a type the inspector knew well. Men of science. Learning for learning's sake. Abstract ideas. A certain austerity in walk and movement, and also in conduct. Contacts in many countries. The kind of man who had a passion for lectures, conferences, and correspondence with colleagues abroad.

Duclos was distinctly nervous, if such a word could

18

be applied to a man whose features hardly ever moved. On the table at which he had been sitting was a bottle of mineral water. Big books and papers were scattered over it.

"I don't see any policeman on guard here."

"I gave them my word of honor I wouldn't leave the hotel. . . . But I should like to point out that I am expected by literary and scientific societies in Emden, Hamburg, and elsewhere. I was booked for a number of lectures before I . . ."

A fair, stout woman appeared, obviously the proprietress, and in Dutch Jean Duclos explained to her who his visitor was.

"I thought I might as well ask for a member of the Police Judiciaire to be sent here, though as a matter of fact, I have every hope of solving the mystery myself."

"Perhaps you'll tell me what you know. . . ."

Maigret, sinking into a chair, ordered:

"A Bols . . . in a large glass, please."

"First of all, here are some plans drawn exactly to scale. They've been made out in duplicate, so I can let you have copies. The first one is the ground floor at the Popingas' — the hall on the left, the living room on the right, the dining room behind. Then right at the back the kitchen, and beyond that the shed where Popinga kept his bicycle, and his boat in the winter."

"You were all in the living room, I think?"

"Yes, all the time—except that twice Madame Popinga and once her sister, Any, went into the kitchen to see about the tea, because the maid had already gone to bed. . . . This is the second floor—at the back, the bathroom, directly over the kitchen. In front, two rooms;

19

to the left, the Popingas' bedroom; to the right, a little study provided with a divan, where Any slept. The other bedroom, over the dining room, had been given to me."

"Show me from which windows the shot could conceivably have been fired."

"From the one in my room, the one in the bathroom, or from the one downstairs in the dining room."

"Tell me just what happened during the evening."

"My lecture went off splendidly. I gave it in this hotel. They have a good room for that sort of thing. Come and see. . . ."

He led Maigret across the hall to a long room, hung with paper garlands, which served also for charity dances, banquets, and amateur theatricals. Behind a platform at one end hung a drop curtain representing the grounds of a chateau.

"Afterward we walked back toward the Amsterdiep," said the professor, leading the way back into the café.

"Along the quay? . . . Will you tell me the exact order in which you walked?"

"I led the way with Madame Popinga. . . . A most cultured woman . . . Conrad Popinga followed, flirting with that little idiot of a farmer's daughter, who can do nothing but grin and giggle, and who certainly didn't understand a word of my lecture from start to finish. Behind them came the Wienands, Any, and that young pupil of Popinga's. A pale-faced, nondescript boy of whom I can tell you nothing."

"You reached the house . . ."

"I daresay you've heard about my lecture. I spoke of the responsibility of criminals for their actions. Ma-

20

dame Popinga's sister, who has just gotten her law degree, and who will soon be practicing, asked me some questions that took us to the subject of the way a lawyer should play his part in a criminal action. Then we discussed scientific methods of detection, and I remember advising her to read the works of the Viennese professor Grosz. I maintained that scientific crime is, under present conditions, undetectable. I spoke at some length on fingerprints, the analysis of all sorts of remains, and the limited deductions that can be made from them. . . . Conrad Popinga, on the other hand, insisted on our listening to the radio."

The shadow of a smile flitted across Maigret's face.

"He got his way, and we had to listen to jazz. Popinga brought out a bottle of brandy and was astonished that a Frenchman could refuse it. He had some; so did that farm girl. They were in very high spirits . . . they danced . . . Popinga was positively exuberant. I heard him say: *'Comme à Paris?'* "

"You didn't like him!" said Maigret.

"There certainly wasn't much in him beyond health and muscle. Wienand was different. Though he specializes in mathematics, he's not narrow, and he had been following our conversation with interest. . . . Then one of the infants began to cry, and the Wienands left. . . . The farmer's daughter was laughing and giggling more than ever. . . . Conrad offered to see her home. They left with this boy they call Cor, with their bicycles. . . . Madame Popinga took me upstairs, and I sat in my room sorting out some papers and jotting down a few notes for a book I am writing. Suddenly I heard a shot. It was so close it might have been in the

21

room itself. . . . I dashed out. The bathroom door was ajar, and I rushed in. The window was wide open. Someone was groaning in the garden near the shed. . . ."

"Was the light on in the bathroom?"

"No . . . I leaned out the window, and as I did so my hand touched the butt of a revolver. Without thinking what I was doing, I picked it up. . . . I could just make out a man's figure lying on the ground. . . . I turned to go downstairs and ran into Madame Popinga on the way. She had heard the shot too, and was in quite a panic. We went down together and were halfway across the kitchen when Any joined us. She was quite beside herself and had come down just as she was . . . in her underwear! . . . That will mean more to you when you get to know her."

"And Popinga?"

"He was dying. He looked at us with big troubled eyes, pressing one hand to his chest. . . . I think he wanted to speak. But the moment I tried to lift him, he stiffened in my arms. . . . He was dead, shot through the heart."

"Is that all?"

"We telephoned the police station and the doctor. And we called Wienand, to come over to help us. . . . I began to sense a certain embarrassment in the air, and I suddenly realized I was still holding the revolver. The police were aware of this and asked me to explain it. Then they politely asked me to hold myself at their disposal."

"That was six days ago, wasn't it?"

"Yes. Since then I've been working on the problem.

It certainly is one! . . . Look at these papers! . . . Yet I feel I'm making progress."

Maigret knocked out his pipe without so much as glancing at the papers.

"You're confined to the hotel?"

"As a matter of fact, I'd rather it was left like that. I wish to avoid any possible incident. Popinga was very popular with his pupils, and it's impossible to go out without running into them at every corner."

"They haven't found any clues?"

"Precious few. But Any brings me any information she thinks might be helpful. She is working on the case too, and has hopes of clearing it up, though to my mind she doesn't go about it quite methodically enough. . . . She told me that the bathtub is provided with a sort of wooden lid which, when down, serves as an ironing board. And the day after the crime, a cap was found lying in the bathtub, a peaked cap like all the sailors wear around here. It had never been seen in the house before. . . . A careful examination of the ground floor, moreover, brought to light a cigar butt on the dining-room carpet. It was very dark tobacco—Manila, I think. Nobody who'd been in the house that night was in the habit of smoking such a thing. As for me, I never smoke at all. . . . And this is the interesting thing: the dining room had been swept directly after dinner."

"From which you conclude?"

"Nothing," answered Duclos dryly. "I'll come to my conclusions in due course. I must apologize for having brought you on such a long journey. But I confess I am surprised they should have sent someone who doesn't speak Dutch. . . . Really, I think there's not likely to

23

be anything for you to do, unless they take action against me that necessitates an official protest."

Maigret ran his finger up and down his nose, smiling a smile that was nothing short of delicious.

"Are you married, Monsieur Duclos?"

"No."

"And until you came here the other day you had never met the Popingas, Any, or anybody else here?"

"We were quite unknown to each other, though of course they knew me by reputation."

"Of course . . . Of course . . ."

Maigret picked up the duplicate plans from the table, stuffed them in his pocket, touched the brim of his hat, and wandered out.

The police station was a modern building, well lit, clean, and comfortable. They were expecting Maigret. The stationmaster had informed them of his arrival, and they were astonished that he had not yet shown up.

He strode in as though he belonged to the place, took off his light coat and threw it and his hat on one of the chairs.

The detective who had been sent over from Groningen to take charge of the case spoke French slowly and just a little pedantically. He was fair and lean, extremely cordial, nodding as he spoke in a way that meant:

"You understand, don't you? I'm sure we can agree."

Though in point of fact it was Maigret who did the talking to start with.

"Since you've been here six days," he said, "you've probably checked all the times?"

"What times?"

"It would be interesting to know, for instance, just how many minutes it took Conrad Popinga to see Mademoiselle Beetje home and return to his house. And then there's another thing: I would like to know the exact time Mademoiselle Beetje went indoors. . . . And also what time young Cornélius went up the gangway of the training ship. I suppose there was a man on watch who would be able to tell you."

The Dutchman looked embarrassed. He got up suddenly, as though an idea had just struck him, went to the other end of the room, and returned with a sailor's cap that looked as though it had weathered more storms than one. Speaking with exaggerated solemnity, he said:

"We've found out who is the owner of this cap. It was found in the bathtub. It belongs to . . . to a man called the Baes. . . . That means something like *the boss*. . . ."

Was Maigret even listening?

"We haven't arrested him, because we thought it better to watch his movements. Besides, he's very popular in the district. . . . Do you know the mouth of the Ems? . . . Approaching from the North Sea, you come to some small sandy islands, which are almost completely submerged by equinoctial tides. They are about seven miles from here. . . . One of them is called Workum, and it's on this island that the Baes lives. He has his family there and some men who work for him. He's taken it into his head to use the place for cattle-breeding. . . . He also gets a small income from the government for running the lighthouse there. He's even been made mayor of Workum, of which he and his

25

people are the only inhabitants. . . . He has a cruiser in which he runs over here to Delfzijl. . . ."

If Maigret was interested, he certainly didn't betray it.

"He's an odd fish — about sixty, hard as nails. And his three sons are each of them as big a pirate as their father. . . . You see . . . Well, it's like this . . . though we don't say much about it; we have to turn a blind eye to it. . . . The ships that come here, as you probably know, mostly carry timber from Riga or Finland. And some of the cargo is stowed on deck. The skippers have orders, if they run into bad weather, to throw some of their deck cargo overboard, in order not to risk the ship. . . . Do you understand what I'm saying?"

Perhaps Maigret did, perhaps he didn't.

"He's a cunning fellow, the Baes. He knows the captains of all the ships that call here, and he can wangle anything with them. They can generally find a pretext to jettison some of their cargo, and the next tide washes it up on the Workum sands. The Baes goes fifty-fifty with the skippers. . . .

"And it's his cap that was found in the bathtub. . . . There's only one thing that doesn't quite fit. He's a pipe smoker. Never smokes anything else. . . . Though, of course, there might have been somebody with him. . . ."

"Is that all?"

"Monsieur Popinga, who has friends all over the place—or who used to have—was, only a fortnight ago, appointed vice consul of Finland at Delfzijl."

The young man looked triumphant. He almost preened with self-satisfaction.

"Where was his boat on the night of the crime?"

The answer was almost shouted:

"At Delfzijl! . . . Alongside the quay! Near the lock! . . . In other words, only about five hundred yards from the house."

Maigret filled his pipe and wandered up and down the room. From time to time he cast a gloomy look at the police reports lying on the desk, of which he could understand not a single word.

"You haven't found out anything else?" he asked, thrusting his hands deep in his pockets.

He was hardly surprised to see the Dutch detective redden.

"You know already?"

Then he corrected himself.

"Of course. You've been the whole afternoon in Delfzijl. French methods, I suppose!"

He spoke awkwardly.

"I really don't know how much importance we ought to attach to it. . . . It was on the fourth day after the crime . . . Madame Popinga came to see us. She said she had been to see the pastor first to know whether she ought to speak. . . . You know the Popingas . . . Not yet? . . . I can let you have the plans."

"Thanks. I have them already," answered the inspector, taking them out of his pocket.

The other was taken aback, but nevertheless went on:

"You see the Popingas' bedroom? . . . From that window you can see only a small part of the path leading to Liewens' farm. Just the part that is lighted up for a moment every fifteen seconds by the lighthouse beam."

27

"And Madame Popinga was watching? Jealous, I suppose."

"Ya. She was watching. She saw the two ride off toward the farm. Then she saw her husband riding back. . . . And then again, only a hundred yards behind him, Beetje Liewens."

"In other words, after Conrad Popinga had seen her home, Beetje followed him back? . . . What does she say about it?"

"Who?"

"The girl . . . Beetje."

"Nothing, so far. I was in no hurry to question her. You see, it's really a very serious matter. And you put your finger right on it when you spoke of jealousy. . . . You see, don't you? . . . And it's not made any easier by the fact that Liewens is on the Council."

"I wonder what time Cor went on board?"

"That I can tell you. We did check. Five minutes past twelve."

"And when was the shot fired?"

"At five minutes to. . . . Only, don't forget there's the cap and the cigar butt."

"Does he have a bicycle?"

"Ya. Everybody bicycles here. It's so convenient. I do myself. . . . But that evening he hadn't taken his bicycle."

"Has the revolver been examined?"

"Ya. It was Conrad Popinga's. A service revolver. It was always fully loaded and kept in one of the drawers of his desk."

"From what distance was the shot fired?"

"About six yards. Exactly the distance from the

bathroom window. . . . But the distance from Monsieur Duclos's window is the same. . . . Then there's nothing to prove that the shot came from upstairs. Judging from the wound, it was fired from above, but Popinga might have been leaning over his bicycle, in which case the line of fire would have been about level. . . .

"Only, there's still that cap in the bathtub . . . and the cigar."

"To hell with the cigar!" muttered Maigret between his teeth.

And then out loud:

"Does her sister know what Madame Popinga told you?"

"Yes."

"What does she say?"

"She says nothing. She's very studious, no chatterbox. She's not like other young women."

"Is she very plain?"

"She's not exactly pretty."

"Right. That means she's plain. . . . You were saying?"

"She wants to discover the murderer. She's working on the case, and has asked to be allowed to look through our reports."

As luck would have it, she came in at that very moment. She was dressed with a severity that might almost be called bad taste. A leather briefcase was tucked under her arm.

She walked straight up to the Groningen detective and began speaking to him volubly in Dutch. Either she didn't notice Maigret or she chose to ignore him.

The Dutchman blushed, shifted from one foot to the other, and fiddled with his papers to cover his embarrassment. He looked up at Maigret to warn her of his presence, but she didn't take the hint.

Finally, in desperation, he said awkwardly, in French:

"She says it's illegal for you to question anybody in Dutch territory."

"Is this Mademoiselle Any?"

Her features were irregular, the mouth too large. Yet if it hadn't been for her teeth, which were very crooked, her face would have been no worse than many others. She was flat-chested and had large feet. But the most striking thing about her was her self-assertiveness.

"Of course, strictly speaking, she is correct. But I'm telling her that it is often done, all the same."

"Mademoiselle Any understands French, doesn't she?"

"I think so."

With her chin in the air, the young woman waited for them to finish as though their conversation did not concern her in the least.

"Mademoiselle," said Maigret, with exaggerated courtesy, "I have the honor to introduce myself. Inspector Maigret of the Police Judiciaire. . . . The only thing I'd like to ask you is what you think of Mademoiselle Beetje and the way she carries on with Cornélius."

She tried to smile. A forced, shy smile. She looked at Maigret and then at the Dutch detective, finally stammering, in painful French:

"I . . . I . . . I don't know what you mean."

No doubt she had never had to speak French before, for with the effort she blushed scarlet to the roots of her hair.

– 3 –

The Quay Rats Club

There were about a dozen of them, men in heavy blue knit smocks, peaked caps, and varnished sabots. Some of them were leaning against the town gate, some sitting on bollards, others simply standing on their two legs, which their wide trousers made enormous.

They smoked, chewed tobacco, and, more than anything else, spat. Now and again someone would make a joke, at which the others would roar with laughter and slap their thighs.

A few yards from them were the boats, and farther off the prim little town, nestling within the circle of its dike. Beyond, a crane was at work, unloading a collier.

Maigret, as he approached the group, had time to observe them, especially when no one noticed him coming along the quay.

He already knew who they were. That is to say, he knew they were the men who were laughingly spoken of as the Quay Rats Club. But even without that information he would have had no difficulty in guessing that

31

the majority of these sailors spent the greater part of their days at the same place, regardless of rain or sunshine, yarning lazily, and bespattering the ground with their saliva.

One of them was the owner of three fine sailing ships of four hundred tons, provided with auxiliary motors. One of these was at that moment beating up the Ems and would, before long, be entering Delfzijl's harbor.

Others were of humbler station. One, a caulker, didn't look as if he had very much to caulk. Another was lockkeeper of a disused lock, but he had, nonetheless, the distinction of wearing a uniform cap.

One, standing in the middle, eclipsed all the others, not only because he was the tallest, broadest, and reddest in the face, but also because his was apparently by far the strongest personality.

Sabots. A smock. The cap on his head was brand-new, and somehow it looked ridiculous, as though it had not yet had time to settle down on its wearer's head.

He was Oosting, more often called the Baes. He was smoking a short-stemmed clay pipe while listening to the talk around him.

A vague smile hung around his mouth. From time to time he would remove his pipe to exhale the smoke with greater relish between almost closed lips.

A minor pachyderm, thick and tough, he had very gentle eyes. In fact, there was, at the same time, something tender and something hard about his whole person.

His eyes were fixed on a boat made fast to the quay, a boat about fifty feet long, of good lines, obviously fast. Probably it had once been a pleasure craft, but was now ill-kept and dirty. It was his.

Beyond it stretched the Ems, twelve or thirteen miles wide, and beyond that again the distant expanse of the North Sea. In one place a streak of reddish sand was Oosting's domain, the island of Workum.

The day was closing in, and the colors of sunset made this little brick town of Delfzijl redder than ever.

Oosting's eyes, wandering gently over the scene, gathered Maigret—so to speak—on the way. The greenish-blue eyes were tiny. For quite a while they remained fixed on the inspector. Then he knocked his pipe on the heel of his sabot, spat, groped for something in his pocket, and produced a tobacco pouch made of a pig's bladder. Shifting his position, he leaned lazily back against the wall.

From that moment, Maigret never ceased to be conscious of the man's gaze trained on him. A gaze in which there was neither arrogance nor defiance. A gaze that was calm, and yet not free from care, and which measured, weighed, and calculated.

The inspector had been the first to leave the police station after his meeting with Any and Pijpekamp—for that was the Dutch detective's name.

Any emerged shortly afterward, walking briskly, with her briefcase under her arm, her body leaning forward, like a woman engaged on some important business who had no time to spare for what went on around her in the street.

Maigret did not bother about her, but watched the Baes. The latter's eyes followed her as she receded into the distance, finally turning back once more to Maigret.

Without knowing exactly why he did so, the inspector went up to the group, among whom all talking ceased abruptly. A dozen faces were turned on him, all expressing some measure of surprise. He addressed himself to Oosting:

"Excuse me! Do you understand French?"

The Baes did not flinch. He seemed to be reflecting. A wizened sailor standing next to him explained:

"Frenchman! . . . French *politie!*"

It was not dramatic, and yet it was one of the strangest minutes Maigret ever lived through. The Baes, whose eyes had rested for a moment on his boat, was obviously hesitating.

There was no doubt about it. He wanted to ask the inspector to go on board his boat with him. It was fitted with a small oak-paneled cabin, in which was a compass and a compass lamp.

Everyone remained stock-still, waiting. Finally Oosting opened his mouth.

Then all at once he shrugged his shoulders, as much as to say:

"It's preposterous."

But those were not his words. In a hoarse voice, which came from right at the back of his throat, he said:

"Pas comprendre . . . Hollandsch . . . English."

Any, wearing her mourning veil, was still visible in silhouette as she crossed the canal bridge and turned along the Amsterdiep.

The Baes caught Maigret looking at the new cap, but it didn't seem to trouble him at all. The shadow of a smile flickered on his lips.

Maigret would have given all he possessed to be able

to talk to this man in his own language, even if it was only for five minutes. In desperation he went so far as to blurt out a few syllables of English, but with such an accent that no one understood a word.

"*Pas comprendre! . . . Personne comprendre! . . .*" said the wizened sailor who had intervened before.

The Quay Rats Club gradually resumed their conversation as Maigret sadly walked off with the feeling that he had come close to the heart of the mystery, but all to no purpose.

A few minutes later he turned around to look at the group, who were still gossiping in the last rays of the setting sun, which made Oosting's red face more inflamed than before.

So far, Maigret had kept—so to speak—to the outskirts of the case, postponing the visit—invariably painful—to a bereaved household.

He rang. It was a little after six. He had not realized that it was a mealtime for the Dutch until he saw, over the shoulder of the little servant who opened the door, two women sitting at the table in the dining room.

They both rose hastily, with prompt but rather stiff politeness. The sort of manners a girl might bring away with her from finishing school.

They were both in black from head to foot. On the table were the tea things, thin slices of bread, and cold meats. In spite of the twilight, the lamps were not lit, the light of a gas fire being left to battle with the gathering darkness.

It was Any who thought of switching on a light in

the living room, telling the servant to draw the curtains.

"I am so sorry to disturb you," said Maigret. "All the more so at mealtime. I didn't know. . . ."

Madame Popinga waved a hand awkwardly toward a chair and looked embarrassed; her sister edged away to the farthest corner.

The room was similar to the one he had been in at the farm. Modern furniture, but of a modernism in no way exaggerated. The soft neutral colors combined somberness with elegance.

"You've come about . . . ?"

Madame Popinga's lower lip quivered, and she had to put her handkerchief to her mouth to stifle a sudden sob. Any did not move.

"I won't bother you now," said Maigret. "I'll come back later. . . ."

With a sign, she insisted on his staying. She was making a valiant effort to regain her composure. She must have been some years older than her sister; she was tall and altogether much more of a woman. Her features were regular, though her cheeks were just a little too florid. In places, her hair was beginning to turn gray.

All her movements were marked by well-bred self-effacement. Maigret remembered that she was a headmaster's daughter, and that she had the reputation of being very cultured and speaking several languages. But all that had not sufficed to make her a woman of the world. On the contrary, her shy awkwardness was thoroughly provincial, and obviously she was the sort of person who would be shocked by the least untoward thing.

He remembered, too, that she belonged to the strictest of Protestant sects, that she generally ran any charity that was organized in Delfzijl, and was also the leading spirit in intellectual circles.

She managed to recover her self-control—though she looked pleadingly at her sister, as though to ask her to come to the rescue.

"You must excuse me, Inspector. . . . It's unbelievable, isn't it? . . . Conrad, of all people! . . . A man who was loved by everybody."

Her eyes fell on the radio in a corner of the room, and at the sight she nearly burst into tears.

"It was his chief amusement," she stammered. "That and his boat, in which he spent summer evenings on the Amsterdiep. He was a very hard worker. . . . Who could have done such a thing?"

Maigret said nothing, and she went on, reddening slightly, in a tone she might have used had she been taken to task.

"I'm not accusing anybody. . . . I don't know . . . that is, I don't want to think . . . It's only the police who thought of Professor Duclos, because he was holding the revolver. . . . I really have no idea. . . . It's too terrible. But there it is—someone killed Conrad. . . . Why? Why him? And not even for robbery . . . Then what could it have been for?"

"You spoke to the police about what you saw from your window?"

She reddened still more. She was standing, leaning one hand on a table.

"I didn't know whether I ought to or not. I don't for a moment think Beetje had anything to do with it. . . . Only, as I happened to look out of the window,

37

I saw . . . And I've heard that the most insignificant details can help the police. . . . I asked the pastor what he thought about it, and he said I ought to speak. . . . Beetje is a good girl. . . . Really, I can't imagine who . . . But whoever it is, it's someone who ought to be in an asylum."

Unlike Beetje, she did not have to grope for her words. Her French was easy, and tinctured with only the faintest accent.

"Any told me you'd come from Paris because of Conrad's death. Is that really so?"

She was much calmer. Her sister, still in her corner, did not move, and Maigret could see only her reflection in a mirror.

"I suppose you'd like to see the house?"

She seemed resigned to it, though she added with a sigh:

"Would you like to go with . . . Any?"

The young woman's black figure stalked past the inspector, and he followed it up the newly carpeted stairs. The house, which could not have been more than ten years old, was lightly built of hollow brick and wood, but it was so well kept and so well painted as to be perfect in its way. Almost too perfect, suggesting an ornament or a model rather than a real home.

The bathroom door was the first to be opened. The wooden cover was lowered over the bathtub, which was thus transformed into an ironing board. Leaning out the window, Maigret saw the bicycle shed, the well-kept vegetable garden, the fields beyond, and the low houses of Delfzijl. Few had more than one story, and not one had more than two.

Any waited in the doorway.

"I hear you're making your investigations too," said Maigret.

She winced, but made no answer, and hastily turned to open the door of the room Duclos had occupied.

A brass bed. A pine wardrobe. The floor covered with linoleum.

"Whose room is this as a rule?"

It cost her an effort to find her words.

"Mine . . . when I stay here."

"Do you come often?"

"Yes . . . I . . ."

It must have been her shyness. The sound seemed to be strangled in her throat. She looked around as though for a way of escape.

"But, since the professor was here, I suppose you slept in your brother-in-law's study?"

She nodded, and opened the door for him to inspect it. A table was filled with books, including some new handbooks on gyroscopic compasses and the control of ships by radio. Sextants. Photographs on the walls showing Conrad Popinga in Asia and in Africa wearing the uniform of first officer or captain.

A divan covered with blue rep.

"And your sister's room?"

"It's the next one."

There was a door leading to it, as well as one leading to the professor's room. The Popingas' room was better furnished than the latter. An alabaster lamp stood at the head of the bed, and the Persian carpet was quite a fine one. The furniture was of some exotic wood.

"And you were in the study . . ." said Maigret dreamily.

A nod from Any.

39

"Which you could only leave by passing through one of the two bedrooms . . ."

Another nod.

"And the professor was in his room, and your sister in hers. . . ."

Any's eyes widened. She opened her mouth, gaping with astonishment.

"You don't think . . . ?"

"I don't think anything," muttered Maigret. "I'm simply investigating, eliminating. And, so far, you're the only person who can be logically eliminated—that is, unless Duclos or your sister is shielding you."

"You . . . you . . ."

But Maigret went on talking to himself:

"Duclos could have fired the shot from either his room or the bathroom. That's obvious. . . . Madame Popinga, for her part, could have fired from the bathroom. But the professor was there within a few seconds, and he saw nobody. . . . When he did see her, she was coming out of her own room a moment or so later. . . ."

Any seemed to be getting over her shyness. These technical considerations seemed to reassure her. The angular half-fledged woman was giving way to the full-fledged graduate in law.

"The shot could have been fired from below," she said, her eyes brightening, her thin body tense. "The doctor says . . ."

"Whatever he says doesn't alter the fact that the revolver that killed your brother-in-law is the one Duclos was holding in his hand. . . . Unless, of course, the murderer threw it up through the bathroom window onto the sill inside."

40

"Why not?"

"Indeed! Why not?"

And Maigret turned, without waiting for her to lead the way, and went down the stairs, which seemed too narrow for him, and whose steps creaked beneath his weight.

He found Madame Popinga still standing, apparently not having moved since he left her. Any followed him into the room.

"Did Cornélius come here often?"

"Nearly every day. He had lessons only three days a week, Tuesdays, Thursdays, and Saturdays. But he'd come just the same the other days. . . . His parents live in India, and it was only a month ago that he learned of his mother's death. She was buried, of course, long before he got the letter. . . . So we tried . . ."

"And Beetje Liewens?"

There was an awkward pause. Madame Popinga looked at Any. Any stared at the floor.

"She used to come. . . ."

"Often?"

"Yes."

"Did you invite her?"

They were getting down to brass tacks. Maigret felt he was making progress, if not toward the solution of the mystery, at any rate in his knowledge of the Popingas' private life.

"No . . . yes . . ."

"She's not quite the same type as you and Mademoiselle Any, is she?"

"She's very young, of course. . . . Her father was a friend of Conrad's. . . She would bring us apples, raspberries, cream."

"Was she in love with Cornélius?"

"No."

The answer was categorical.

"You never cared much for her, did you?"

"Why shouldn't I? . . . A jolly girl: whenever she came she'd fill the house with her chatter and laughter. More like the chirping of a bird, if you know what I mean."

"Do you know Oosting?"

"Yes."

"Was he a friend of your husband's?"

"Last year he had a new engine put in his boat, and he asked Conrad's advice about it. In fact, Conrad drew up some plans for him. And they used to go seal-shooting together on the sandbanks."

She hesitated a moment before suddenly blurting out:

"You're thinking of the cap, perhaps. . . . You think he might have . . . Oosting! . . . It's impossible."

She heaved a sigh and then went on:

"No. I can't believe it's Oosting either. I can't believe it's anybody. Nobody could have wanted him to die. . . . You never knew him. . . . He . . . he . . ."

Weeping, she turned her head away. Maigret thought it better to go. They didn't offer to shake hands, so he simply bowed his way out, muttering excuses.

Outside, he was surprised by the chill dampness that rose from the canal. On the other bank, not far from the shipwright's yard, he caught sight of the Baes talking to a young man in uniform, evidently one of the cadets from the training ship.

They were standing together in the twilight. Oosting was apparently speaking emphatically. The young man hung his head. Maigret could only just make out the pale oval of his face, but he at once jumped to the conclusion that it was Cornélius. And when he saw a crepe band on his sleeve, he felt quite sure.

−4−

Floating Logs

There was nothing clever about it, nor was anything done furtively. From start to finish, Maigret never had the feeling he was spying on anybody.

He had walked out of the Popingas' house and taken a few steps. Seeing the two figures on the other side of the canal, he had stopped quite naturally to look at them. He didn't attempt to conceal himself. There he was, standing right on the bank of the canal, his pipe between his teeth, his hands in his pockets.

But if he was not hiding, he was nevertheless unseen. The conversation on the other bank continued earnestly. Yes—there was no doubt about it—they were quite oblivious of his presence. There could be no doubt either about another thing: whatever was being discussed was something of the gravest importance. And whether it was the tone of voice or the emphasis given to the words, there was something tense, even something touching, about the scene.

Or perhaps it was the setting. There was no one

else on the other bank of the canal. It was deserted. A shed was standing in the middle of the shipwright's yard, where two boats lay cradled on dry land.

In the canal itself were the floating logs, so many that it was only in the middle that a narrow strip of water was visible, a yard or two in width. The evening was advancing. The air was beautifully clear, and there was just enough light left for colors to have their full value.

So intense was the calm that it was almost unbelievable. The croaking of a frog in a distant pond broke through it so harshly as to be positively startling. Yet on the opposite bank neither of the two men seemed to notice it.

The Baes went on talking. He didn't raise his voice, but in his quiet way he nevertheless hammered out the syllables. Either he was taking great pains to make himself understood, or he was giving orders in such a way as to ensure their being obeyed. With lowered head, the cadet listened. He wore white gloves, which struck two sharp notes in the otherwise quiet scene.

Suddenly there was a rending cry. It was a donkey braying in the meadow behind Maigret. This was enough to break the spell. Oosting looked toward the animal, and as he did so he noticed Maigret. For a moment he gazed steadily at him, apparently not in the least disconcerted.

Turning back to the boy, he wound up his discourse with a few final words; then, stuffing the short stem of his clay pipe into his mouth, he walked off toward town.

What had they been talking about? In all probability it was something far removed from the case Maigret was on. Had the people of Delfzijl nothing else to talk about than the death of Conrad Popinga? . . . And yet . . . Maigret went on wondering.

Oosting's path soon branched off from the canal, and he disappeared behind some sheds, though for a good minute the sound of his sabots could clearly be heard.

Lamps were being lit in town and along the canal as far as the Wienands' house, where they ended. There were no houses on the other bank, which was fast melting into shadows.

Maigret turned to look back without knowing why. He growled an oath as the donkey once more rent the heavens.

In the distance, beyond the last of the houses, he caught sight of two little white spots dancing over the canal. They were Cor's gloves.

It would have been a weird sight, those hands waving over the water, the body lost in the semidarkness, if Maigret had not remembered the logs.

Oosting's steps were now out of earshot. Maigret walked back toward the last of the houses, once more passing the Popingas' and then the Wienands'.

He was still taking no pains to conceal his presence, but he knew very well that his figure, like Cor's, must be indistinguishable from the shadows. More than Cor's, since he had no white gloves.

He watched those gloves crossing the canal. He understood. To avoid going all the way around by Delfzijl, where there was a bridge over the canal, the boy had gone straight from bank to bank, using the logs as stepping-stones. In the middle, he might have had as much as five or six feet to jump.

Cor was now on the same bank as Maigret, walking barely a hundred yards in front of him. Maigret followed.

It might have been accidental; it might have been instinctive. In any case, it wasn't done on purpose. But the fact remains that Maigret's footsteps crunching on the cinder path were exactly in step with the other's.

Maigret tripped over something, and for a fraction of a second the unison was lost. It was only then that he became aware that he was dogging Cor's footsteps like a bloodhound. He had no idea where he was being led. When the boy quickened his pace, he quickened his too. He was beginning to feel a sort of giddy passion of pursuit.

At first the stride had been long and regular. Little by little the steps had shortened and quickened. Just as Cor passed the lumberyard a whole orchestra of frogs struck up, and he stopped dead.

Was he frightened?

On again. But the steps were now more irregular. Sometimes one foot seemed to hesitate in the air. At other moments Cor took two or three steps so rapidly that it looked as though he was going to break into a run.

The silence was now definitely over. The frogs never stopped their croaking, which filled the night.

The pace was getting still hotter. By marching in step with the boy, Maigret even became conscious of his frame of mind.

Yes, Cor was afraid. He was hurrying because he was afraid. He was itching to be back on board, or wherever it was he was going to. But each time he passed the shadow of a bush, a dead tree, or a pile of lumber, there was a slight hesitation in his step.

There was a bend in the canal. A hundred yards farther on toward Liewens' farm was the little space that was lit up by the lighthouse. It seemed to make the young man vacillate still more. He cast a glance over his shoulder, ran past the place, then looked back again.

He was now well beyond it, and it was Maigret's turn to enter the lighted area. Cor looked back a third time.

This time it was impossible for him not to notice the inspector, whose large bulky figure marched purposefully through the beam. Cor stopped, but only long enough to take a breath. Then he was off again.

The light was behind them. In front, a lighted window, one of the windows of the farm. The song of the frogs seemed to be following them. They had walked a considerable distance since it first started, yet it was now as close as ever. It seemed as though the frogs were all around them, hundreds of them, escorting them on their way.

When Cor stopped next, there was no hesitation; it was a decisive halt. He was barely a hundred yards from the house. A figure emerged from behind a tree. A voice spoke in a whisper.

Maigret did not want to turn back. It would have been too ridiculous. Nor did he want to hide. Besides, it was too late to hide, now that he had passed through the beam from the lighthouse. They knew he was there. He walked forward slowly, disconcerted that his steps no longer had an accompaniment.

It was very dark here; leafy trees hemmed in the towpath from each side. But a white glove was visible. Was it holding something? Or pressing something to him? . . .

Yes; they were embracing. Cor's arm was around Beetje's waist.

He was only fifty paces from them. Maigret stopped, felt for his matches, and struck one, ostensibly to light his pipe, but really to give official notice of his presence.

Then he went on. The couple stirred. When he was ten yards away, Beetje's figure detached itself from Cor's. She came forward and stood in the middle of the path, looking in Maigret's direction as though waiting for him. Cor remained leaning against the trunk of the tree.

Maigret had almost reached them. The window in the farm was still lighted. A simple rectangle of reddish light.

Suddenly a cry—raucous, indescribable—a cry of fear, of exasperation—one of those cries that usher in a fit of sobbing or a flood of tears.

It was Cor. His head was in his hands as he stood cowering against the tree. He was sobbing.

Beetje was right in front of Maigret now. She was wearing a coat, but the inspector noticed that beneath it was her nightgown. Her bare feet were in slippers.

"Don't take any notice of him."

Beetje was perfectly calm. She even threw Cor a reproving, impatient glance.

Turning his back on them, the latter tried to pull himself together. He was ashamed to be seen in such a state, yet he could not control it.

"He's upset. . . . He thinks . . ."

49

"What does he think?"

"That he's going to be accused of . . ."

The young man kept his distance. He was drying his eyes. Was he on the point of taking to his heels? His attitude certainly suggested it.

"I haven't yet accused anybody," said Maigret, for the sake of saying something.

"Exactly . . ."

And, turning toward the boy, she said something in Dutch, the purport of which Maigret could only guess.

"You see! The inspector's not accusing you. For heaven's sake calm down. It's childish to go on like that. . . ."

She broke off abruptly, standing still, listening. Maigret had heard nothing, but a few seconds later he thought he could make out the faintest of footfalls in the direction of the farm.

It was enough to bring Cor to his senses. He looked around, his face haggard.

No one spoke.

"Did you hear?" whispered Beetje.

The young man was on the point of advancing to the spot from which the sound seemed to come. All at once he was game as a fighting cock. He was breathing deeply.

He was too late, however. The enemy was much closer than they had supposed. A few yards off, a figure emerged from the darkness, a figure immediately recognizable as the farmer Liewens. He was shod in nothing but his socks.

"Beetje!" he called.

At first she didn't dare answer. But when he repeated the name she tamely said:

50

"Ya."

Liewens came closer. He passed Cor, whom he ignored. Perhaps he had not yet noticed Maigret.

Nevertheless, it was in front of the inspector that he finally stopped, his eyes hard, his nostrils quivering with rage. He held himself in, however, standing perfectly still. When he spoke, he turned toward his daughter.

His voice, though subdued, was rasping. Two or three phrases, while she stood before him hanging her head. Several times he repeated the same word in a tone of command. Finally Beetje said, in French:

"He wants me to tell you . . ."

Her father was watching her as though wanting to satisfy himself that she translated his message faithfully.

". . . that in Holland policemen are not in the habit of meeting girls at night in the dark."

Maigret blushed. Such a blush as he rarely experienced. A flood of hot blood that made his ears hum.

It was such an absurd accusation. So obviously malicious. For there was Cor, and her father must have known very well that it was for him that Beetje had left the house.

But he was helpless. What could he answer? . . . Particularly when everything he said had to pass through an interpreter.

As a matter of fact, no answer was expected. At least, none was waited for. The farmer snapped his fingers, as one might to recall a dog, and pointed toward the path leading to the house. Beetje hesitated, turned to Maigret for a moment, but finally walked away without daring to cast a glance at her lover. Liewens followed.

Cor had not moved. He did raise a hand as though

51

to stop the farmer, but it was a futile gesture and he let it fall again. Father and daughter disappeared into the darkness, and a moment later their front door slammed.

Had the frogs held their peace during this little scene? Maigret couldn't be sure. He had forgotten all about them. But now their croaking seemed all at once positively deafening.

"Do you speak French?"

Cor did not answer.

"Do you speak French?"

"Petit peu . . ."

He glared at Maigret, and was obviously reluctant to open his mouth. He stood sideways, as though to offer less target to an attack.

"What is it you're so afraid of?"

Tears ran down the boy's cheeks again, though no sobs came. He blew his nose, taking a long time over it. His hands were trembling. He looked as though he might at any moment break down again.

"Do you really think that you're suspected of having killed the teacher?"

And in a gruff voice Maigret added:

"Come on. Let's go. . . ."

He swept the boy off toward town. When he started talking, he did not economize on words, because he had the feeling the boy understood barely half of what he was saying.

"Was it on your own account that you were frightened?"

A mere boy! A thin face, with pale complexion and features still unformed. Narrow shoulders in his tightly

52

fitting uniform. And his cadet's cap dwarfed him, making him look like a child dressed up in a sailor suit.

His face and every gesture showed mistrust and resentment. If Maigret had raised his voice, he would no doubt have thrown up an arm to ward it off.

The crepe armband struck another, still more pathetic, note. Wasn't it only a month ago that the boy had learned of his mother's death in India? . . . One evening, perhaps, when he had felt especially carefree? Perhaps the night of the training ship's annual ball?

In two years' time he would leave to rejoin his remaining parent, having attained the rank of third officer. And his father would take him to see a grave already weathered . . . and perhaps introduce him to a new mother installed as lady of the house. . . .

Then his career would begin, on a liner or a big cargo boat. Standing watch. Rotterdam to Java. Java to Rotterdam. Ports of call. Two days in one place; in another only five or six hours . . .

"Where were you at the moment Conrad Popinga was killed?"

The sob burst now—a terrible rending sob. With his white-gloved hands, the boy caught hold of the lapels of Maigret's coat—hands that shook convulsively.

"Not true! . . . *Pas vrai!*" he repeated at least ten times. *"Nein! . . .* You don't understand. . . . *Pas . . . Non! . . . Pas vrai!"*

Again they passed into the beam from the lighthouse, which blinded them, threw them sharply into relief, down to the smallest detail, then swept on, leaving them once more indistinguishable from the night.

"Where were you?"

"Not there."

Not there. "There" meant the Popingas' house, and the little part of the canal he used to jump across with the help of the logs.

This last was a detail that was certainly not unimportant. It might even be very serious. Popinga had been shot at five minutes to twelve, and Cor had reported on board at five minutes past. Taking the ordinary route—that is to say, going around by way of the town—he would have needed nearly half an hour. But only six or seven minutes by taking his shortcut from bank to bank.

Maigret walked on ponderously beside this flimsily built cadet who was trembling like a leaf. The donkey brayed again, which only made things worse. He shook from head to foot, and once more seemed on the point of taking to his heels.

"Do you love Beetje?"

An obstinate silence.

"You saw her go back, after Popinga had seen her home, didn't you?"

"It's not true. . . . *Pas vrai! Pas vrai!*"

Maigret was tempted to shake him. That might have calmed him and brought him to his senses. Instead, he looked at him with an indulgent, almost affectionate eye.

"Do you see Beetje every day?"

Once more no reply.

"What time are you supposed to be back on board?"

"Ten o'clock . . . except with special permission . . . When I go for private lessons . . . I could . . ."

"Get back later. But that evening you had no lesson, did you?"

They were on the bank of the canal, just where Cor had jumped across. In the most natural way, Maigret turned toward the canal and stepped onto one of the logs, nearly falling into the water when it rolled over under his weight.

Cor hesitated.

"Come on. It's nearly ten."

The boy was surprised. He must have expected never to set foot on the training ship again, to be arrested, thrown into prison. . . .

But now this fearsome French detective was leading him home. They crossed together, jumped together when they came to the gap in the middle, splashed each other. On the other bank Maigret stopped to wipe his trousers with his handkerchief.

"Where is it?"

He hadn't yet been on this side. It was a nondescript stretch of land between the Amsterdiep and the new canal, which was wide and deep enough to carry oceangoing ships.

Looking back, the inspector saw a lighted window upstairs in the Popingas' house. Silhouetted against the blind was Any's figure. It must be Conrad's study. Maigret stared, but it was impossible to guess what Any was doing.

Cor was a little calmer now.

"I swear . . ." he began.

"No, don't!"

That disconcerted him. He looked at his companion with such alarm that Maigret patted him on the shoulder as he said:

"Swearing doesn't do any good. Particularly in your position . . . Would you like to marry Beetje?"

"Ya! . . . Ya! . . ."

"Would her father give his consent?"

Silence. With lowered head Cor walked on, picking his way between numerous old boats left here to rot.

Soon a large expanse of water came into sight. The Ems Canal. At a bend, a large black-and-white ship raised its masts into the night. The forecastle was very high. All the portholes were lighted.

It was an ancient Dutch man-of-war, at least a hundred years old, that had been moored in the canal to finish its days in peace and quiet as a training ship.

Nearby on the shore were dark figures and many glowing cigarettes. The distant sound of a piano could be heard, no doubt, from the gun room.

Suddenly a bell pealed, and in a moment the dark figures scattered on the bank had clustered into a swarm at the foot of the gangway. A few who had wandered farther came up at the double.

They were just like a crowd of schoolboys, though they ranged in age from sixteen to twenty-two, and wore the uniform of officers in the merchant service: white gloves, stiff, gold-braided peaked cap.

At the top of the gangway, leaning over the side rail, an old quartermaster watched them pass one by one as he quietly smoked his pipe.

The whole scene was alive with youthfulness and high spirits. Jokes were told and laughed at, though naturally they were lost on Maigret. Cigarettes were thrown into the water as the cadets stepped on board. There they went on with their fun, skylarking, teasing, and chasing each other around the deck.

The last stragglers, panting, were going up the gangway. Cor, his features drawn, turned toward the inspector. His eyes were red and feverish.

"Get along with you!" growled Maigret. *"Allons, va!"*

The boy understood the tone rather than the words. His hand went to his cap in an awkward salute. He opened his mouth to speak. . . .

"That's all right. . . . Go on. Run!"

The quartermaster was already leaving the top of the gangway. One of the cadets was taking over the watch.

Through the portholes they could be seen unlashing their hammocks and tossing their clothes onto their sea chests.

Maigret stayed where he was until he saw Cor join them. The boy went down the ladder shyly and awkwardly, his shoulders hunched and crooked, and threaded his way toward one of the end hammocks. Before he got to it, he had received a flying pillow full in the face.

The inspector had not taken ten steps toward town when he caught sight of Oosting, who, like him, had been watching the cadets return on board. They were both adults and big, heavy, and placid. Wasn't it rather absurd that they should have been watching that crowd of young men and boys climbing into their hammocks and engaging in pillow fights? Didn't it make them look like two old hens, watching over a too-adventurous brood of chicks?

They looked at one another. The Baes did not flinch.

With a leisurely movement he touched the peak of his cap.

They knew perfectly well that conversation between them was impossible. All the same, the mayor of Workum couldn't help saying:

"Goed avond . . ."

"Bonne nuit . . ." echoed Maigret.

They were taking the same road, a road that, after about two hundred yards, became a street of the town.

They were walking almost abreast. To avoid doing so, one of them would have had deliberately to slacken his pace. And neither wanted to.

Oosting, in his sabots. Maigret, in his city clothes. One with a clay pipe between his teeth, the other with a brier.

The third house they came to was a café, and Oosting went in after shaking the mud off his sabots, which, in any case, he left at the entrance, according to Dutch custom.

Maigret hardly hesitated a second. He, too, went in.

There were about ten men inside, sailors and bargees, sitting around the same table, smoking pipes and cigars, drinking beer and gin.

Oosting shook hands with some of them; then, seeing an empty chair, he sat down heavily and listened to the talk.

Maigret sat down too, keeping his distance from the others. Though nobody ostensibly took any notice of him, he knew very well he was the center of interest. The proprietor, who was one of the group, waited a few moments before coming over to him to ask him what he wanted.

The schnapps was drawn from a porcelain tap with brass fittings. It was that which gave the place its pervading odor, as it did in every other café in the Netherlands, and which was so different from any café in France.

Oosting's small eyes twinkled every time they lighted on the inspector.

The latter stretched out his legs, tucked them under his chair, then stretched them out again. He filled his pipe. Anything to cover his embarrassment. The proprietor got up again on purpose to give him a light.

"Moïe veer!"

Maigret frowned, and, with a gesture, showed he could not understand.

"Moïe veer, ya! . . . Oost vind . . ."

The others listened, nudged each other. One of them pointed through the window to the starry sky outside

"Moïe veer! . . . Bel temps!"

He was trying to explain that the wind was from the east, which brought good weather.

Oosting was choosing a cigar from a box that had been set before him. For all the world to see, he deliberately took a Manila black as coal, the end of which he bit off and spat on the floor.

He called the attention of the others to his new cap.

"Vier gulden . . ."

Four florins. Maigret worked out what that would be in French money. Oosting's eyes never stopped twinkling.

But someone entered, and, unfolding a newspaper, started talking about the latest prices on the Amsterdam Bourse.

The conversation that followed was animated. Indeed, it sounded more like a quarrel, owing to the loud voices and the harshness of the Dutch tongue. Maigret was forgotten. He fumbled in his pocket and produced some small change. Then he went off to the Hotel Van Hasselt, where he went to bed.

– 5 –

The Professor's Theories

Sitting downstairs over his breakfast in the Hotel Van Hasselt, Maigret could watch, through the window, the Dutch police getting to work. They had not told him their intentions, but they couldn't be blamed for that, considering how short a time he had given them the day before. If he had gone his own way, he could hardly complain if they went theirs.

It must be about eight o'clock. The morning mist had not yet been dispersed, though there were signs of a bright sun somewhere behind it. A tug was towing a Finnish ship out of the harbor.

At one end of the quay, a crowd of men was gathered in front of a small café, talking in little groups. All wore sabots and peaked caps.

They were the *schippers*, and it was apparently there that they did their business. Their barges and boats of every description, crawling with women and children, filled up one basin of the port.

Farther on was another group, but only a handful: the Quay Rats Club.

Two uniformed policemen had just arrived and gone on Oosting's boat. The latter had emerged from the cabin, for when he was in Delfzijl he always slept on board.

Another man, in plainclothes, joined them. It was Pijpekamp, the Groningen detective in charge of the case. He raised his hat and politely addressed the Baes, while his two men disappeared below.

The search began. All the *schippers* were conscious of what was going on. Nevertheless, there was no crowding around, nor any other outward sign of curiosity.

Nor did the Quay Rats Club betray any excitement. A casual glance or two was all they conceded.

The work went on for a good half hour. Then the policemen reappeared, saluted the detective, and reported the results of their labors. Pijpekamp offered what looked very much like an apology.

The Baes seemed quite unmoved, though he apparently wasn't inclined that morning to join his acquaintances on shore. Instead, he sat down on the roof of the cabin and, crossing his legs, stared out to sea, to where the Finnish ship was slowly diminishing in the distance.

Maigret had been watching it all. When at last he looked back into the room, it was to see Jean Duclos coming downstairs with an armful of books and papers and a fat briefcase, which he laid out on the table that had been set aside for him.

He did not trouble to say good morning, but merely asked:

"Well?"

"Very well indeed, thank you. And I hope it's the same with you."

The professor looked up with surprise, then shrugged his shoulders as though he had come to the conclusion that it really wasn't worthwhile taking offense.

"Have you found out anything?"

"Might I ask if you have?"

"You know very well that I can't set foot out-of-doors. Your Dutch colleague, however, has had the good sense to realize that my technical knowledge might be of service. I am accordingly kept informed of how the investigation is proceeding . . . an example that might well serve as a lesson for the French police."

"Of course!"

The professor jumped to his feet as Madame Van Hasselt entered the room, her hair in curlers. He bowed to her in his best company manner, and though he spoke in Dutch, Maigret could have bet anything he was inquiring after her health.

The inspector looked at the papers spread out over the professor's table. There were fresh plans and diagrams, not only of the Popingas' house, but of almost the whole town. There were arrows, which no doubt indicated the route followed by some person or persons.

The sun streaming through the stained-glass windowpanes threw patches of green, red, and blue light on the varnished woodwork. A brewer's dray had drawn up outside, and throughout the conversation that followed, two burly giants rolled barrels across the floor, supervised by Madame Van Hasselt in her slippers. The smell of schnapps and beer lay thick in the air. This was Holland—and Maigret had never felt it so keenly.

"You've discovered the murderer?" he asked blandly, pointing to the papers.

A sharp, hostile look from Duclos, as he answered:

"I'm beginning to think that foreigners are right when they think French people incapable of being serious. . . . In the present circumstances, Monsieur, your playfulness is not in the best of taste."

Not in the least disconcerted, Maigret smiled serenely, while the professor went on:

"No. I have not discovered the murderer. But I have done something that is far more useful at the start than merely looking for the murderer. I've analyzed the case. Dissected it, so to speak. I have all the elements neatly sorted out. And now . . ."

"And now?"

"It will no doubt be someone like you who will reap the reward of my deductions."

He sat down. He was determined to discuss the case even in this hostile atmosphere, for which he had only himself to thank. Maigret sat down opposite him and ordered a glass of Bols.

"Fire away."

"First of all, please note the fact that I am not asking what *you* have done, nor what you think about the case. . . . And now I begin with the first suspect, that is to say, myself. I occupied the best strategic position, if I may so express myself, from which to kill Popinga. Moreover, I was seen holding the revolver that had shot him, a few moments after it had been fired.

"I am not rich, and if my name is known all over,

64

or nearly all over, the world, it is by a small number of intellectual people. I live in a circumscribed manner, and it is not always easy to make ends meet. . . . On the other hand, there was no robbery; nor was I likely to benefit in any way from Popinga's death. . . .

"But, wait a moment. That does not mean that I couldn't have committed the murder. There are people who can tell you that in the course of the evening, during a discussion of scientific police methods, I had been arguing that an intelligent man who, with a cool head, used all his ingenuity, could perfectly well elude detection by the police, half-educated as the latter are. . . . And it could quite well be maintained that I had a bee in my bonnet as regards this subject to the extent of wanting to prove my theory in practice. On the other hand, you will perhaps appreciate the fact that, had I committed a perfect crime and gone unsuspected, I should have proved my point to no one but myself. And you will admit when you know me better that I am not the man to do anything so foolish. . . ."

"Here's luck," said Maigret, lifting his glass, at the same time watching the bull-necked brewers' men as they rolled their casks across the floor.

"On the other hand, suppose I did not commit the crime, but that it was committed—as everything seems to indicate—by another member of the household. In that case, one must come to the conclusion that everybody in the house is implicated.

"That surprises you, no doubt. But look at this plan. . . . And there are various psychological considerations I must explain to you, and which I hope you will be able to follow."

Maigret smiled more blandly than ever at the professor's patronizing tone.

"No doubt you have heard of Madame Popinga's family. The Van Elsts belong to the most austere sect of the Protestant church. In Amsterdam her father passes for an extreme conservative, and her sister, Any, though she is only twenty-five, is already taking up politics and following in his footsteps.

"You have not yet been here twenty-four hours, and one can hardly expect you to understand the manners and customs of this place. There are many things that would surprise you. You would hardly guess, for instance, that an officer on the staff of the training ship would be severely reprimanded if he was seen to enter a café—even a respectable place like this. One of them was dismissed because he persisted in taking a newspaper that is considered rather advanced. . . .

"I saw Popinga only that one evening. But it was enough, particularly after what I'd heard about him. . . . A good fellow, you would call him, no doubt. That's the expression invariably used for people of his type. I don't say he did not have his good qualities. Of course he had. Suppose we put it this way:

"He'd been a sailor, he'd been all over the world. Then he'd come to roost here, and they had put him in a straitjacket. Only, it was bursting at every seam.

"Do you understand? I suppose you will smile at what is to follow. A Frenchman's smile! . . . A fortnight ago he went to the weekly meeting of his club. Those who can't go to a café get around it by forming clubs. A special room is reserved for them, where they can play billiards or ninepins.

"As I was saying, Popinga went to his club. And by eleven o'clock that evening he was drunk. . . . That same week his wife was taking up a collection to buy clothing for some natives or other. And Popinga, his cheeks red and his eyes shining, was heard to say: 'What nonsense it all is! They're very well off as they are. Instead of buying clothes for them, we'd do better to follow their example, and go naked too.'

"You smile—I knew you would. You think it's trivial. But that doesn't alter the fact that his words made a scandal that has not yet died down, and if his funeral takes place in Delfzijl there will be a good many absentees.

"That's only a detail, but it's one of a hundred others, of a thousand others. As I said, it was every seam that was bursting, and through the cloak of respectability the real Popinga was showing.

"To drink a glass too much is by itself a matter of the utmost gravity. And don't forget Popinga's pupils used to see him in that state. . . . That's why they adored him, of course.

"With that in mind, try to reconstruct the atmosphere of that house beside the Amsterdiep. Think of Madame Popinga, of Any. . . .

"And now look out the window. With one sweep of your eye you can take in the whole town from one end to the other. Delfzijl is a very small place. Everybody knows everybody else. The least little scandal, and there's not a soul who doesn't know it.

"Then who should Popinga choose to make a friend of but the Baes? A man who, if the truth be told, is nothing less than a pirate. They used to go out shooting seal together, and they'd drink schnapps together in the cabin of the boat. . . .

"Now don't jump to conclusions. Just bear in mind what I said—that if the crime was committed by anybody in the house except me, then we're all implicated.

"There remains that stupid little Beetje, whom Popinga never failed to see home. I'll mention only one detail: her bathing suit. Everybody else's has a kind of skirt at the bottom. But hers—oh, no! As tight fitting as possible, and red into the bargain! . . .

"And now I leave you to pursue your own investigations. I merely wished to make you aware of a few factors, which are of the kind the police usually ignore. . . .

"As for Cornélius Barens, I consider him one of the family, and if I am not mistaken, he belongs to the Van Elst side of it.

"The characters in this case range themselves naturally into rival sides, so to speak. On the one hand, Madame Popinga, her sister, Any, and Cornélius. On the other, Popinga, Oosting, and Beetje.

"Think it over, and perhaps you may even come to some useful conclusions."

"One question . . ." said Maigret gravely.

"Yes?"

"You're a Protestant, too, I think?"

"I certainly belong to the Reformed Church, though not to the same branch as Madame Popinga."

"Which side are you on?"

"I did not care for Popinga!"

"So you . . . ?"

"I deplore the crime, regardless of the victim."

"He listened to jazz and danced, didn't he, while you were talking to the ladies?"

"Yes. That was characteristic of him, though I didn't take it as a personal affront."

Maigret was magisterially serious as he got up, saying:

"All in all, who would you advise me to arrest?"

The professor bridled.

"I didn't speak of arresting anybody. I have simply given you certain guidelines. We have been dealing with generalities."

"Admittedly. But in my place . . . ?"

"I am not a member of the police! I pursue truth for truth's sake, and the fact that I have come under suspicion myself doesn't affect my judgment in the slightest."

"So I oughtn't to arrest anybody?"

"I didn't say that either. . . . I . . ."

"Thank you," said Maigret, offering his hand.

He wanted to pay for his Bols, and to call attention he struck his glass with a coin. Duclos looked at him disapprovingly.

"That's not done here," he murmured. "At least, not if you wish to pass for a gentleman."

They were closing the trapdoor through which the barrels of beer had been lowered into the cellar. The inspector paid, and, throwing a last look at the plans, he said:

"So it comes to this: either it's you, or all the family."

"I didn't put it quite like that. . . . Listen . . ."

But Maigret was already at the door. Now that his

69

back was turned, he allowed his features to relax from the gravity he had assumed during the last part of the conversation. If he didn't actually laugh, he certainly went out beaming.

The quay outside was bathed in sunshine, gentle warmth, and peacefulness. The ironmonger was standing on his threshold. The little man who kept the chandler's shop was counting his anchors and marking them with signs in red paint.

The crane was still busy unloading coal. The *schippers* hoisted their sails, not because they were putting to sea, but to dry the canvas. Some white, some brown, they hung flapping lazily among the crowd of masts.

Oosting smoked away at his short-stemmed clay pipe, sitting in his boat. The Quay Rats Club went on with their leisurely discussions.

Turning his back on that scene to study the town, he was faced by well-built, well-painted houses, windows beautifully clean, curtains spotless, cactuses on every windowsill. But what was behind those windows?

Certainly they looked different now, after the conversation Maigret had had with Duclos. The latter was no fool, for all his pedantry. There were, indeed, two worlds here.

One, the saltwater world. Men in sabots, boats, sails, the smell of tar . . . and schnapps.

The other, the world of respectability. Houses that seemed hermetically sealed, in whose rooms, with their well-polished furniture and somber wallpaper, they had for the last fortnight been shaking their heads over a certain officer from the training ship who had had one or two glasses too many.

The same sky hung over both worlds, a sky limpid

as in a dream. But that didn't make any difference: the two worlds were separated by an almost impassable border.

Maigret had never seen Popinga, nor even his body, but it was not difficult to picture him. A man with a jolly, rubicund face, which betrayed human appetites.

And he could see him standing, so to speak, astride this border, looking enviously at Oosting's boat, at the five-master whose crew had been having a fling in every South American port, or at the Dutch liner home from China, where you could find whole junk-loads of girls, pretty as hell. . . .

Whereas all he was allowed was an English dinghy, well varnished, with fittings of polished brass, in which he might on summer evenings go rowing on the flat waters of the Amsterdiep, threading his way through logs that had come from the far north or from equatorial forests.

The Baes was now looking at Maigret, and the latter could not help thinking that the man would like to speak to him. But it was out of the question. They hadn't half a dozen words in common.

Oosting knew how hopeless it would be, and remained sitting where he was, his eyes half closed against the brightness of the sun. The only sign of his frustration was that he smoked a little more quickly.

Cornélius Barens would, at that hour of the morning, be sitting in a classroom trying, perhaps, to grasp some lesson on spherical trigonometry. He probably looked like a washed-out rag.

The inspector was about to sit down on a bronze bollard when he noticed Pijpekamp coming toward him, holding out his hand.

"Did you find anything in the boat this morning?"

"Nothing . . . But we had to carry out the search as a matter of form."

"Do you suspect the Baes?"

"There's the cap. . . ."

"And the cigar!"

"No. The Baes only smokes a pipe. If he does smoke a cigar once in a while, it's never a Manila."

Pijpekamp drew Maigret farther on, to be out of range of Oosting's eyes.

"The compass on board once belonged to a Swedish ship, and the life preservers to an English collier. . . . It's like that with practically everything on board."

"Stolen?"

"Not exactly. At any rate, not stolen by him. When a ship arrives, there's generally somebody, an engineer, a third officer, a deckhand, or even sometimes the captain, who's got something to sell. . . . Do you see? . . . The things are logged as washed overboard or broken. . . . In one way or another, almost anything can be written off, even navigation lights! Of course, with a boat it's easy. . . ."

"So there's nothing unusual about it?"

"Nothing at all. The man who has that chandler's shop there gets half his goods that way."

"Where does that bring us then?"

The Dutchman looked the other way. He seemed embarrassed.

"I told you that Beetje Liewens did not go straight indoors when she reached her house, but followed Popinga back. . . . Am I making myself clear? You must tell me when I make mistakes."

"Yes, yes. Go on."

"Though of course that doesn't necessarily mean she fired the shot. . . ."

"Ah!"

Pijpekamp was certainly far from being at ease. He drew Maigret still farther on, to a part of the quay that was deserted. Then, lowering his voice, he said:

"You know that pile of lumber, don't you? . . . The *timmerman*—I suppose you'd call him a carpenter—well, he says he saw Beetje and Monsieur Popinga that evening . . . together. . . ."

"Having a kiss in the dark, I suppose?"

"Yes . . . And it seems to me . . ."

"What?"

"If one person saw them, others might. . . . That young man from the training ship, for instance—Cornélius Barens. He wants to marry Beetje. We found a photograph of her among his things."

"Really?"

"And then Liewens—Beetje's father . . . He's a very influential man, a cattle-breeder in a big way, exporting even as far as Australia. He's a widower, and she's his only child. . . ."

"So he might have killed Popinga?"

The Dutchman was so ill at ease that Maigret almost took pity on him. It obviously cost the man a colossal effort to harbor suspicions against such an important man, who could export cattle all the way to Australia.

"If he saw them . . . mightn't he have . . . ?"

But Maigret was merciless.

"If he'd seen what?"

"Seen them by the pile of lumber . . . Beetje and Popinga."

"Ah! I see."

73

"Of course, this is absolutely confidential."

"Naturally . . . And Barens?"

"He could have seen them too. And he could hardly help being jealous. . . . Still, there's no doubt about one thing, he was back on board ten minutes after the crime. That seems to clear *him*, all right. But still . . . all the same . . ."

"So it comes to this," said Maigret, in the same serious way he had spoken to Duclos, "your suspicions are centered on Beetje's father and this boy, Cor."

An awkward silence.

"Though you also suspect Oosting, who left his cap in the bathtub."

Pijpekamp looked discouraged.

"And then, this unknown man who left the butt of a Manila cigar in the dining room . . . How many tobacconists are there in Delfzijl?"

"Fifteen."

"That certainly doesn't help matters. . . . And, last, you suspect Professor Duclos."

"With that revolver in his hand, I really couldn't let him go. . . . You understand, don't you?"

"Oh, yes, I understand."

They walked on for fifty yards without anything further being said.

"What do you think about it?" muttered the Groningen detective at last.

"Ah! That's just it. And that's just the difference between us. You've got an idea—in fact a lot of ideas—whereas I don't yet think anything at all."

A sudden question:

"Does Beetje Liewens know the Baes?"

"I don't know. I don't think so."

"Does Cor know him?"

Pijpekamp drew his hand across his forehead.

"Perhaps . . . perhaps not. . . . On the whole, I think not. But I could find out."

"Do. Try to find out if they had anything to do with each other before the crime took place."

"You think . . . ?"

"I tell you I don't think anything. But here's another question: Has the Baes a radio set on that island of his?"

"I've no idea."

"It might be worthwhile finding out."

It was difficult to say how it had come about, but the case seemed to have slipped out of the Dutchman's hands and into Maigret's. At all events, the look Pijpekamp turned on the inspector was very much like a subordinate's.

"You might look into those two points. There's someone I must go and see. . . ."

Pijpekamp was too polite to ask who it was, though his eyes betrayed his curiosity.

"Beetje Liewens," said Maigret. "Which is the shortest way from here?"

"Along the Amsterdiep."

The Delfzijl pilot boat, a fine vessel of five hundred tons, turned in a wide circle on the Ems, then headed toward the port.

The Baes was on his feet now, pacing up and down his little deck with slow heavy strides that betrayed inward tension. A hundred yards from him the Quay Rats Club basked lazily in the sun.

$-6-$

The Letters

Along the Amsterdiep, Pijpekamp had said; but for no particular reason Maigret didn't follow his instructions. Instead, he went across the fields.

In the eleven o'clock sun, the farm reminded him strongly of his first visit there, the girl in her shiny black boots in the up-to-date cowshed, the well-furnished living room, and the teapot standing under its cozy.

The scene was just as quiet today. The limitless horizon breathed peace. It was uninterrupted except for one big red-brown sail. He gazed at it across the fields. It seemed altogether unreal, floating in the sky, almost as though it were sailing over an ocean of grass.

The dog barked at him, just as it had the first time. It was a good five minutes before the door opened, but even then it was opened only an inch or two, just enough for him to catch a glimpse of the servant's florid face and her checked apron.

She was on the point of shutting it again when Maigret hastily asked:

"Mademoiselle Liewens?"

The door opened a little wider. And the servant's head emerged. The garden was between them, since Maigret had remained standing at the gate. Between them was the dog, baring its teeth as it kept watch on the intruder.

The servant shook her head.

"Isn't she here? . . . *Niet hier? . . .*"

Maigret had managed to pick up one or two words of Dutch.

But the servant only shook her head more emphatically.

"And the master? . . . *Mijnheer? . . .*"

One more head-shake, and the door was shut. But Maigret did not go, and as he stood staring at the house he saw the door move again, though this time only a fraction of an inch. The old servant was no doubt peeping at him.

But what really made him stand there was that he had seen one of the curtains move, and he knew that that curtain belonged to Beetje's room. It was difficult to see through it, but there was certainly a face there. What Maigret saw more clearly was a slight movement of a hand, a movement that might have been no more than a greeting. But Maigret thought it meant more:

"I'm here. . . . Don't insist. . . . Look out!"

Six pairs of eyes were on him. The old servant's behind the door, Beetje's through the curtain, and the dog's. The latter jumped up against the gate, barking. Around them, in the fields, the cows stood so still it was difficult to believe they were alive.

Maigret thought he'd try a little experiment. He was

standing two or three yards from the gate; and he suddenly took two paces forward, exactly as though he was going to jump over it. He couldn't help smiling, for not only was the door closed hurriedly, but also the dog slunk back toward the house with its tail between its legs.

With that, the inspector left, taking the towpath along the Amsterdiep. All he could gather from the welcome he had received was that Beetje was shut up in her room, and that orders had been given that he was not to be admitted.

Thoughtfully he puffed away at his pipe. He looked for a moment or two at the piles of logs and lumber under the shadow of which Beetje and Conrad Popinga would stop—often, no doubt—and, holding their bicycles with one hand, embrace.

Over all hung this even calm. Such quiet, such serenity—it was almost too perfect, so perfect that it was difficult for a Frenchman to believe that life here was life at all. Was it? Or was it all as flat and artificial as a picture postcard?

Everything seemed strange to Maigret. For instance, turning suddenly, he saw, only a few yards from him, a high-stemmed boat he had not seen arriving. He recognized the sail, which was broader than the canal, as the one he had seen only a little earlier far away toward the horizon. It seemed hardly possible that it could have covered the distance in so short a time.

At the helm was a woman, who steered with a hip against the tiller while she held a suckling baby to her breast. A man was sitting astride the bowsprit, his legs dangling down toward the water, fitting a new martin-gale.

The boat passed in front of the Wienands' and then the Popingas'. The mast reached higher than the roofs, and the sail completely blotted out each house in turn.

Maigret stopped again. He hesitated. The Popingas' servant was scrubbing the doorstep, her head down, her stern in the air. The door was open.

Suddenly realizing that someone was behind her, she scrambled hastily to her feet, so nervous that her hand shook.

"Madame Popinga?" he asked, pointing toward the interior of the house.

She wanted to go in first, but she hesitated, not knowing what to do with the wet cloth she was holding, which was dripping dirty water. Maigret took advantage of her embarrassment and went straight in. Hearing a man's voice behind the living-room door, he knocked.

The voice broke off abruptly. Dead silence in the room. As a matter of fact, it was more than silence; suspense would be the better word.

At last there were steps, and a hand touched the door handle; the door slowly opened. The first person Maigret saw was Any. It was she who had opened the door, fixing him with a hard stare. Next he made out the figure of a man standing near the table. His suit was of thick broadcloth. Liewens, the farmer.

Last, he saw Madame Popinga, leaning against the mantelpiece, her face buried in her hands.

It was obvious that the newcomer was interrupting

some important conversation, a tense discussion, or a dispute.

The table was covered by an embroidered cloth, on which letters lay scattered, as though they had been flung down in anger or indignation.

The farmer's face showed every sign of strong emotion. But he quickly got his feelings under control, and his features set into cold, hostile reserve.

"I'm afraid I am interrupting you . . ." began Maigret.

No one answered. No one said so much as a word. Then Madame Popinga, after a wild look around, rushed out of the room and hurried off to the kitchen.

"I am really very sorry to have broken in upon you like this."

At last Liewens spoke. Turning to Any, he rapped out a few phrases in Dutch, and the inspector could not help asking:

"What does he say?"

"That he'll come back another time. . . . That it's high time . . ." She broke off, not knowing quite how to put it.

Maigret came to her rescue.

"That it's high time the French police were taught manners! Something like that, wasn't it? . . . We've run into each other before, this gentleman and I."

The farmer was trying to understand the gist of Maigret's words by watching his features and listening to his intonation.

Meanwhile, the inspector's eye had wandered to the letters on the table. He caught sight of the signature at the bottom of one: Conrad.

The atmosphere became tenser. The farmer went

over to a chair and picked up his cap. Then he paused. He couldn't, after all, make up his mind to go.

"I suppose he's brought you the letters that your brother-in-law wrote to his daughter?"

"How did you know?"

Good gracious! Wasn't it obvious enough? One could hardly imagine a scene that was easier to reconstruct. The atmosphere was thick with it. . . . Liewens arriving panting, trying to hold in his fury. Liewens shown into the living room, politely asked to take a seat by the two frightened women. But instead of sitting down bursting out with all his pent-up wrath, flinging the letters down on the table . . .

Madame Popinga, not knowing what to say, not knowing what to do, hiding her face in her hands, inwardly refusing to believe the evidence that was spread out before her eyes . . .

And Any, feebly arguing, trying to hold her own against the angry farmer.

That was where they'd got to when Maigret knocked, and they'd all stood, still as statues, till Any had walked stiffly over to open the door.

But the inspector's reconstruction was not so accurate as all that. On one point he was wrong. Madame Popinga had more fight in her than he supposed. He had imagined her collapsed in the kitchen, a nerveless wreck. But the next moment she was back in the room, in the state of outward calm that is possible to some people when they are strung up to the highest pitch of emotion.

Slowly, she, too, laid some letters on the table. She

did not throw them down. She laid them down. She looked at the farmer and then at the detective. Two or three times she opened her mouth before she was able to utter a sound, but when at last she did, she spoke quietly:

"Someone must judge. . . . You must read these letters. . . ."

Instantly the farmer's face flushed scarlet. He was too controlled to pounce on the letters, but he seemed almost dizzy with the effort to hold himself back.

A woman's writing . . . elegant blue paper . . . Unmistakably, they were the letters Beetje had written to Conrad.

One thing struck the eye at once: the disproportion in number between hers to him and his to her. The latter could hardly have amounted to more than ten. They were written on a single sheet, and were generally no more than four or five lines in length.

Beetje's letters must have been three times that number. They were long and closely written.

Conrad was dead. There remained this unequal correspondence, and the stacks of lumber that had witnessed their meetings on the banks of the Amsterdiep.

"We must proceed calmly," said Maigret. "There's no use reading these letters in anger."

The farmer looked at him so acutely that Maigret felt sure he understood. He took a step toward the table.

Maigret leaned over it too. At random he picked out one of Conrad's letters.

"Will you be kind enough to translate it for me, Mademoiselle Any?"

But the girl didn't seem to hear. She merely stared at it. Finally her sister took it from his hand.

"It was written from the training ship," she said, with dignity. "There is no date, only the time, six o'clock, and then:

> "My little Beetje,—It would be better if you did not come this evening because my chief is coming for a cup of tea with us.
> "Till tomorrow. Love."

Madame Popinga looked around with an air of calm defiance. She picked up another letter. Slowly she read:

> "Pretty little Beetje,—You must calm yourself. Life is long and there's lots of time ahead. I have a lot of work on hand just now because of the exams. I won't be able to come this evening.
> "Why are you always accusing me of not loving you? You don't expect me to give up the training ship, do you? What could we do?
> "Don't get excited. We have plenty of time before us. With an affectionate kiss . . ."

Maigret waved his hand as much as to say that they had heard enough. But Madame Popinga picked up another letter.

"There's this one," she said. "I think it must be the last he wrote.

> "My Beetje,—It's quite impossible. Do please be reasonable. You know I have no money and that it might take ages to find a post abroad.
> "Don't let yourself get so worked up. You

must have confidence in the future. Everything will come out all right.

"Don't be frightened. If what you fear happened, I wouldn't let you down.

"I'm afraid I am rather irritable because I have so much work to do, and when I think of you, work goes badly. Yesterday I was hauled over the coals about something, and I'm rather upset about it.

"I'll try to get off tomorrow evening on some pretext or other."

Madame Popinga looked from one to the other of the people standing around her. Her eyes were dim. She looked tired, dead tired. But she stretched out her hand toward the other pile of letters, the ones she had brought in herself. The farmer winced.

She picked up the first one she touched and, opening it, read:

"Dear Conrad, whom I love,—Here's some good news for you. As a birthday present Papa has put another thousand florins into my bank account. That's enough to take us to America, for I have looked in the paper to see how much it costs. We could go third class, couldn't we?

"But why aren't you more anxious to be off? I live for nothing else. Everything in Holland is suffocating to me. And I can't help thinking that the people in Delfzijl already look at me in a disapproving way.

"At the same time I'm immeasurably happy and so proud to belong to a man like you.

"We absolutely must be off before the holidays, because Papa wants me to spend a month with him in Switzerland, and I don't want to. If we don't get off soon, we'll be stuck here till the winter.

"I've bought some English books, and I already understand quite a lot of words.

"Quick! Quick! There's a marvelous life for the two of us. Don't you think so? I'm sure of it. We can't stay here any longer. It would be worse than ever now. I think Madame Popinga hates the sight of me, and I am bothered to death by Cor, who won't leave me alone. Try as I do, I can't shake him off. He's a nice boy, such good manners. But what a fool!

"Besides, he's only a boy. So different from you, who have been all over the world and know so many things.

"Do you remember—it's just a year ago now—when we met for the first time? And you didn't even look at me.

"And to think that now I may be going to have a baby—and it will be yours. At any rate I could.

"But why are you so cool? You're not getting tired of me, are you?"

The letter was not yet finished, but Madame Popinga's voice had become so weak that finally she broke

off. She fumbled for a moment among the pile of letters, apparently looking for a particular one.

Having found it, she plunged straight into the middle
of it, reading out:

> ". . . and I am beginning to think that you're
> fonder of your wife than of me. I'm beginning
> to be jealous of her, to hate her. Otherwise, why
> do you refuse to take me away at once?"

All this had been translated into French, of which
the farmer did not understand a word, but his attention was riveted so closely on what she was reading that
he seemed to guess the sense.

Madame Popinga swallowed, then picked up another sheet. Her voice was firmer as she went on:

> "I've heard it said that Cor is more in love
> with Madame Popinga than with me. And they
> really do seem to hit it off perfectly together. If
> only things could develop along those lines!
> Wouldn't that be a magnificent solution? Our
> consciences would be clear."

The sheet of paper slipped from her hand, gliding
down to rest on the floor at Any's feet. She merely stared
at it vacantly, and once more there was silence in the
room.

Madame Popinga was not weeping, but she was
nonetheless a tragic figure—made tragic by her controlled suffering, by her dignity purchased at the price

of intense effort, and made tragic, too, by the exalted emotion that governed her.

She was defending her husband's good name. She waited for a further attack, bracing herself to meet it.

"When did you discover those letters?" asked Maigret, not without embarrassment.

"The day after he was . . ."

She choked, opened her mouth to gasp. Her eyelids swelled.

"The day after . . ."

"Yes. I understand."

Maigret looked at her with pity. She was not beautiful, though she had quite good features, without any of the blemishes that ruined Any's looks.

She was tall, full of figure without being stout. A fine head of hair framed a face that, like so many Dutch women's, was highly colored.

But many an ugly face had more charm, more piquancy. Over her face an immense dullness was written. In it was no trace of impulsiveness. Her smile was a wise, measured smile, and if she ever experienced joy, it could only be wise and measured joy.

At the age of six she must have been a model child. At sixteen she must have been just what she was today—one of those women who seem born to be sisters or aunts, nurses or nuns, or widows busying themselves with charities.

Conrad was gone, yet Maigret had never been so conscious of the man's vitality, his ruddy jovial face, his eagerness to taste all the good things of life—and yet, with his timidity, his fear of hurting anybody's feelings. Conrad turning the knobs of his radio set, wistfully switching from Parisian jazz to Hungarian Gypsy music or Viennese musical comedies, or even picking up messages in Morse from ships on the high seas. . . .

Any went over to her sister, as though the latter was in need of comfort or support. But, waving her aside, Madame Popinga took two or three steps toward the inspector.

"It had never entered my mind," she said, hardly above a whisper. "Never! . . . I was living . . . in such peace . . . and then, at his death, to find . . ."

He guessed from the way she was breathing that she suffered from some disease of the heart. The next moment she confirmed it by standing motionless with a hand pressed to her chest.

Someone moved. It was the farmer, a hard, wild look in his eye, who went to the table and started gathering up his daughter's letters, nervously, like a thief who's afraid he'll be interrupted.

Madame Popinga did not attempt to stop him. Nor did Maigret.

When he had them, he did not turn to go. He began speaking, though he did not seem to be addressing anybody in particular. More than once Maigret caught the word *Franzose,* and it seemed to him that he could at that moment understand Dutch, just as Liewens had apparently been understanding those letters that had been translated into French.

What he heard, or thought he heard, was:

"Do you really think it's necessary to tell all this to a Frenchman?"

His cap dropped to the floor. He stooped to pick it up, bowed to Any, who was between him and the door—

but to her only—and went out, muttering a few words that probably no one understood.

The maid must have finished washing the doorstep, for they could hear the front door open and shut, then steps fading away.

In spite of her sister's presence, Maigret began questioning Madame Popinga again, speaking with a gentleness of which he would hardly have thought himself capable.

"Had you already shown those letters to your sister?"

"No. But when that man . . ."

"Where were they?"

"In a drawer of his desk. A drawer I never opened. I did know he kept his revolver there."

Any said something in Dutch, and Madame Popinga, speaking listlessly, translated:

"My sister tells me I ought to go to bed. I haven't had a wink of sleep these last nights. . . . He would never have gone. . . . Perhaps he lost his head for a moment, but it was never more than that. He liked to laugh; he loved games. . . . All sorts of things come back to me that I took no notice of at the time. Everything looks different now. Beetje coming with fruit and cakes she'd made herself. I always thought they were for me. . . . Then she'd come and ask us to play tennis. Always at a moment when she knew I'd have something else to do. I didn't see it. I didn't want to think evil, and I was so glad for Conrad to have some fun. . . . You see, he worked so hard, and I knew he must find Delfzijl rather dull. . . . Last year, she nearly went to Paris with us. And it was I who pressed her to."

She spoke simply, and with such lassitude that there was hardly room for any rancor.

"He didn't want to leave me. You understand, don't you? . . . He never wished to hurt anyone. Never . . . More than once he got into trouble by marking exams too generously. My father was always holding that against him."

She adjusted the position of an ornament on the mantelpiece, a trivial homely gesture, which seemed altogether incongruous under the circumstances.

"Now, all I want is to know that it's over. They haven't yet given permission for him to be buried. . . . You understand, don't you? I don't know how to explain it. . . . Let them give him back to me, and God can punish the murderer."

She was getting worked up. Her voice rang out more clearly.

"Yes. That's what I believe. . . . Things like that— what can we know about them? All we can do is to leave them to God."

She shivered as an idea suddenly struck her. Pointing outside, she went on breathlessly:

"Perhaps he'll kill her. . . . He's capable of it. . . . That would be awful."

Any looked at her with a touch of impatience. No doubt she considered all this a waste of words. In a calm voice she intervened:

"What do you think about the case now, Inspector?"

"Nothing!"

She did not pursue the question, but she looked annoyed.

"You see," went on Maigret, "there's Oosting's cap.

We mustn't forget it. You've heard Professor Duclos's views, haven't you? . . . And you've no doubt read the works of Grosz, which he talks about. . . . One rule above all others: never let yourself be lured by psychological considerations. Keep to the material evidence and follow wherever it may lead you, right to the end."

It was impossible to tell whether he was sneering or serious.

"And there they are: a cap and the butt of a cigar. Someone brought them here, or threw them in from outside."

"I can't believe that Oosting . . ." began Madame Popinga, speaking more to herself than the others.

Then, suddenly looking up, she went on:

"That reminds me of something I had forgotten. . . ."

But she broke off, as though afraid of having said too much, afraid of the effect her words might have.

"What is it?"

"Nothing. Nothing of any importance."

"Do tell us. Please."

"When Conrad used to go seal-shooting on Workum . . ."

"Well?"

"Beetje went with them. She was always ready for anything like that. And here in Holland we allow girls a lot of liberties."

"Were they away for the night?"

"Sometimes a night, sometimes two . . ."

She waved a hand as though trying to drive the vision away.

"No! . . . I mustn't think of it. It's too awful . . . too awful."

Now the tears came welling up. The sobs were there ready to tear her apart. But before they came, Any placed her hands on her sister's shoulders and pushed her gently out of the room.

− 7 −

Pijpekamp's Luncheon

When Maigret arrived at the hotel, he sensed at once that something unusual was afoot.

The evening before, he had had dinner at the table next to the professor's. But now three places had been laid on the round table in the middle of the room. The tablecloth was snowy white and the creases had not yet gone flat. Moreover, three glasses had been set for each person, and that was a thing done only on grand occasions in Holland.

As soon as he crossed the threshold, the inspector was greeted by Pijpekamp, who came forward with outstretched hand. The smile on his face was that of a man who has a pleasant surprise in store.

He was dressed in his very best. A collar that seemed to be three inches high. A formal coat. He was closely shaved, and appeared to have come straight from the barber's hands; the place reeked of violet hair tonic.

The Dutchman's good spirits were not shared by Jean Duclos, who stood behind him looking ill-at-ease.

"You must excuse me, Inspector," said Pijpekamp, glowing. "I ought to have let you know beforehand. . . . I would like to have invited you to my home, but Groningen is some way off. Besides, I'm a bachelor. So I thought we'd better have it here. Nothing formal, of course. Just a little *déjeuner* together . . . the three of us."

As he spoke he looked at the table with nine glasses. Obviously he was expecting Maigret to make some protest.

But no protest came.

"I thought that, since the professor was a countryman of yours, you would be glad to . . ."

"Of course! Of course!" said Maigret. "Just a moment, while I wash my hands."

He washed them slowly, with a sulky look on his face. From the lavatory, he could hear people bustling about in the kitchen, and the clatter of plates and saucepans.

When he rejoined the others, Pijpekamp himself was pouring out the port. With an ecstatic smile on his face he murmured modestly:

"Just what you do in France, isn't it? . . . *Prosit!* . . . Or, I should say, *Santé, mon cher collègue.*"

He was quite touching. He meant so very well. He trotted out the most elegant phraseology he could find in French, anxious to show himself a man of the world to his fingertips.

"I ought to have invited you yesterday. But I was so—what shall I say?—so upset by this business. . . . Have you found out anything?"

"Nothing!"

There was a little sparkle in the Dutchman's eye, and Maigret thought:

Ah, my fine fellow! You've got a trump up your sleeve, and you're going to play it over the dessert. . . . That is, if you can hold yourself in that long.

He wasn't wrong.

First came tomato soup, and with it Saint-Emilion. The wine had certainly been doctored for export, and was so sweet as to be positively sickly.

"*Santé!*" toasted Pijpekamp once again.

Poor Pijpekamp! He was doing his utmost to play the host properly. More than his utmost. Yet Maigret didn't seem to appreciate it. Didn't even seem to notice it!

"In Holland we never drink with meals, only afterward. In the course of the evening—that is, at large receptions—they serve a small glass of wine with the cigars. . . . Another point on which we differ from you: we never put bread on the table."

He looked proudly at the chunks of bread he had had the foresight to order, and equally proudly at the bottle of port, which stood in the center of the table. He had chosen it with great care, to take the place of the native schnapps.

What more could he have done? He had left no stone unturned to provide all the requisites for a pleasurable meal. Looking tenderly at the Saint-Emilion, he grew quite pink. Duclos ate in silence, his thoughts apparently elsewhere.

Really, it was a shame these two Frenchmen couldn't enter the spirit of it. Pijpekamp had looked forward to this lunch as one that would be sparkling with wit, with verve, with élan, and all the other things he could think of as being preeminently Parisian.

He had, nevertheless, considered that a national dish would be proper to the feast. So *hutschpot* was brought on, the meat swimming in an ocean of sauce. With an arch expression he said:

"You must tell me what you think of it."

But no! Maigret was not in the right mood. As a matter of fact, he was genuinely preoccupied, trying to guess what it was all about. Certainly there was a mystery here somewhere.

Of one thing he felt pretty sure. There was a kind of secret understanding between the Dutch detective and Jean Duclos. Every time his host filled his glass, he seemed to cast a significant glance at the professor.

The burgundy was warming beside the stove.

"I expected you to be much more of a wine drinker. Don't you drink much wine?"

"It all depends. . . ."

Another thing that was certain was that Duclos was far from feeling happy about it. He took little part in the conversation. He sipped rather nervously at his mineral water, having refused wine on the grounds that he was dieting.

Pijpekamp was finding it very hard work, though not so much to keep the ball rolling—for the wine helped him there—as to prevent its rolling too far. It would spoil the effect if he played his trump too soon. It was hard to wait, but he held out for quite a long time. He spoke of the beauty of the harbor, of the amount of traffic carried by the Ems, of the University of Groningen, where the greatest scholars in Europe came every year to lecture.

Then at last:

"By the way," he said, trying to sound casual, "I have some news for you. . . ."

"Really?"

"Your health, Inspector! And health to the French police force! . . . Yes, there's some news to tell you. In fact, I might say that the mystery is practically solved. . . ."

Maigret looked at him stolidly with eyes in which there was not the faintest trace of either excitement or curiosity.

"At ten o'clock this morning I was told that some-one wanted to see me. Who do you think it was?"

"Cornélius Barens. . . . Go on."

It was too bad! Pijpekamp was thoroughly crestfallen to see his trump producing so little effect upon his guest. And after all the trouble he had taken!

"How did you know? . . . I suppose someone told you?"

"Nothing of the sort! What did he want?"

"You know him, don't you? A shy boy. Secretive, I think. He couldn't look me in the face, and he seemed, the whole time, on the verge of tears. . . . He confessed that when he left the Popingas' house he did not go at once on board the training ship."

Pijpekamp was regaining confidence with the sound of his own voice. He looked knowingly at Maigret, and in a more confidential tone went on:

"Do you see? . . . He's in love with Beetje. So he was jealous, because Beetje had been dancing that evening with Popinga. And he was annoyed with her for drinking a glass of brandy.

"He watched them leave together, then followed

97

them a short way, though, of course, being on foot, he was soon outdistanced. He waited there for Popinga to return. . . ."

Maigret was merciless. He knew perfectly well that the Dutchman would give anything in the world for some sign of astonishment or admiration. But his face betrayed neither.

"Cornélius took a little coaxing, because he was afraid, but finally he told me everything. And here it is: Immediately after the shot was fired, he saw a man run toward the stacks of lumber and take cover there."

"I suppose he described the man minutely?"

"Yes."

Pijpekamp's recovery had been short-lived. He looked dejectedly at Maigret, having lost all hope of seeing him taken aback. His well-prepared surprise was nothing but a damp squib.

"A sailor, a foreigner. Tall, thin, clean-shaven."

"And there was a boat, no doubt, that left next morning?"

"Three have left since then," said Pijpekamp, struggling on as bravely as he could. "It really clears the case up, as far as we are concerned. There's no longer any point in looking for the murderer in Delfzijl. . . . Some foreigner killed him. Probably a sailor who'd known Popinga when he was at sea. Perhaps somebody who served under him, and who had an old score to pay off."

Jean Duclos looked woodenly at the opposite wall, avoiding Maigret's eye. Madame Van Hasselt, in her best clothes, was sitting at the cash desk. Pijpekamp made a sign to her to bring another bottle.

The meal was not over. On the contrary, its crowning triumph was only now brought on: a cake garnished with three different creams and, the final touch, the name Delfzijl in chocolate letters.

The Dutchman modestly lowered his eyes.

"Perhaps you would like to cut it. . . ."

"Did you arrest Barens?"

Pijpekamp started, staring at Maigret as though the latter had taken leave of his senses.

"But . . . what for?"

"If you have no objection, we might question him together presently."

"It can easily be arranged. I'll telephone to the training ship."

"While you're about it, you might also arrange for Oosting to be brought along. We'll have some questions for him, too."

"About the cap? . . . That's easily explained now. A sailor, passing his boat, saw the cap lying on the deck. It wouldn't take him a second to pinch it."

"Of course not."

Pijpekamp could have wept. Maigret's sarcasm, though it wasn't laid on thick, was unmistakable. In his agitation, Pijpekamp bumped into the side of the door as he went into the telephone booth.

The inspector was left alone with Duclos, whose eyes were now glued on his plate.

"While you were about it, you might have told him to slip a few florins discreetly into my hand."

The words were spoken quite gently, without any bitterness at all. Duclos raised his head, and opened his mouth to protest.

"Come, come! We don't have time to argue about it. . . . You told him to give me a good meal and plenty to drink with it. You told him that that was the way to get around officials in France. . . . Please don't interrupt. . . . And that after that he could do just as he liked with me."

"I assure you . . ."

But Maigret, lighting his pipe, turned toward Pijpekamp, who was returning from the telephone. Looking at the table, the latter stammered:

"You won't refuse a little glass of brandy, will you? They have some good stuff here."

"If you don't mind, it's my turn now," said Maigret, in a tone that tolerated no opposition. "Only, since I don't speak Dutch, I must ask you to order it for me. A bottle of brandy and some glasses."

Pijpekamp meekly interpreted:

"Those glasses won't do," Maigret said when Madame Van Hasselt came bustling up.

He got up and went himself to get some bigger ones. Placing them on the table, he filled them right up to the rim.

"A toast for you, gentlemen," he said gravely. "The Dutch police!"

The stuff was so strong it brought tears to Pijpekamp's eyes. But Maigret, with a smile on his face, gave no quarter. Again and again he raised his glass, repeating:

"Your health, Monsieur Pijpekamp! . . . To the Dutch police!"

And then he added:

"What time are you expecting Cornélius at the police station?"

"In half an hour . . . May I offer you a cigar?"

"Thanks, I'd rather smoke my pipe."

Once more Maigret filled up the three glasses, doing it with such authority that neither Pijpekamp nor Duclos dared say a word.

"It's a lovely day," he said two or three times. "I may be greatly mistaken, but somehow I have the impression that before the day is out poor Popinga's murderer will be under lock and key."

"Unless he's steaming across the Baltic," answered Pijpekamp.

"Oh! . . . Do you really think he'd be as far as that?"

Duclos turned a pale face to the inspector.

"Is that an insinuation?" he asked acidly.

"What would I be insinuating?"

"You seem to suggest that, if he isn't far, he might be very close indeed."

"What an imagination you have, Professor!"

It might easily have degenerated into a quarrel. Perhaps the large glasses of brandy had something to do with it. Pijpekamp was scarlet, his eyes glistening.

It took Duclos another way; its effect on him showed outwardly as morbid pallor.

"A final glass, gentlemen, and then we'll go and put that wretched boy through the hoop."

He picked up the bottle again. With each glass he poured out, Madame Van Hasselt moistened the point of her pencil, and jotted them down in her book.

Leaving the hotel, they plunged into an atmosphere heavy with peace and sunshine. Oosting's boat was in its place.

They had only some three hundred yards to go. The streets were deserted. So were the clean, well-stocked shops, which looked like the booths of some international exhibition just about to open its doors.

Pijpekamp seemed to find it necessary to hold himself much more stiffly than usual. Summoning all his faculties in a last despairing effort, he turned to Maigret and said:

"It will be almost impossible to find the sailor, but it's a good thing we know it's him, for it clears everybody else of suspicion. . . . I'll be making a report, and as soon as that's done there ought to be no objection to the professor's going on with his lecture tour."

He strode into the Delfzijl police station with more than a suspicion of a stagger, bumping against a table and then sitting down far too emphatically.

Not that he was actually drunk. But the alcohol had deprived him of that smoothness and gentleness that characterize the majority of Dutchmen.

He waved an arm, pressed a button, then tilted his chair. The bell was answered by a policeman in uniform, to whom he gave some brief orders. The man disappeared, returning a moment later with Cor.

Pijpekamp received him with almost exaggerated cordiality, but that did not in any way reassure the boy, who, the moment he caught sight of Maigret, felt the ground sink from beneath his feet.

"There are a few little points we'd like to get cleared up," said Pijpekamp in French, "and my colleague would like to ask you one or two questions."

Maigret was in no hurry. He walked quietly up and down the room, puffing away at his pipe, before saying:

"Look here, Barens, my boy! . . . What was it the Baes was talking to you about last night?"

The cadet turned his thin face this way and that, like a frightened bird.

"I . . . I think . . ."

"Good! Perhaps I'd better help you. You have a father, haven't you? Somewhere out in India, I think. . . . It would be a fearful blow to him if anything happened to you, if you got into trouble in any way. . . . I don't know what it might be, but, in a case like this, perjury, for instance, would be a very serious offense. . . . It would mean prison."

Cor stood rigid now, not daring to move, not daring to look at anybody, hardly daring to breathe.

"Oosting was waiting for you last night by the Amsterdiep. . . . Now, confess that it was he who put you up to it, who told you to tell the police what you've told them. . . . Come on! Out with it! . . . You never saw a tall, thin man near the Popingas' house, did you?"

"I . . . I . . ."

But he hadn't the strength to go further. He crumpled up and burst into tears.

Maigret looked first at Duclos, then at Pijpekamp, with that ponderous, impenetrable stare that sometimes led people to take him for a fool. It was a stare that was so utterly stagnant as to seem empty.

"You think . . . ?" began Pijpekamp.

"What can one think? Look at him!"

The contrast between Cor's unformed figure and the uniform he was wearing made him appear almost childlike. He was blowing his nose and trying to hold back his sobs. At last he succeeded in stammering:

"I haven't done anything."

103

No one spoke for a moment. All eyes were watching his struggle to get control of himself.

"I never said you'd done anything," said Maigret at last. "Oosting asked you to pretend you'd seen a stranger near the house. . . . I suppose he told you that was the only way to save some person. . . . Who?"

"I swear . . . by all that's holy . . . he didn't say who. . . . I don't know. I haven't the least idea. . . . I wish I were dead."

"Of course you do. At eighteen one often wishes one were dead. . . . Have you any further questions, Monsieur Pijpekamp?"

The latter shrugged his shoulders in a way that showed he was quite out of his depth.

"That's all right, little one! You can run along now."

"It's not Beetje, anyhow. . . ."

"I daresay you're right. But now be off with you and get back on board."

And he pushed him roughly, but not unkindly, out of the room.

"Now for the other," he growled. "Is Oosting here? . . . If only he could speak French!"

The bell was rung again, and soon the policeman brought in the Baes, who held his new cap in one hand and his pipe in the other.

He threw a look, a single look, at Maigret. Strangely enough, it was a look of reproach. Then he walked up and stood in front of Pijpekamp's desk.

"If you wouldn't mind asking him . . . Where was he when Popinga was killed?"

Pijpekamp translated. Oosting replied with a long

rigmarole, which Maigret could not get the hang of at all. But that did not prevent him cutting in with:

"No. Stop him! I want an answer in three words."

When that was translated, there was another reproachful look from the Baes.

"He was on board his boat," said Pijpekamp, translating the reply.

"Tell him it isn't true."

Maigret paced up and down, his hands clasped behind his back.

"What does he say to that?"

"He swears he was."

"All right. In that case, he can tell you how his cap was stolen."

Pijpekamp was now merely an interpreter. He was docility itself. But he hadn't much choice. Maigret gave such an impression of power that there was no question of taking the lead out of his hands.

"Well?"

"He was in his cabin. He was doing his accounts. Looking through a porthole in the coaming of the coach roof, he saw the legs of someone standing on deck. Trousers. Sailor's trousers . . ."

"Did he follow the man?"

When that question reached him, Oosting hesitated, with half-closed eyes. Then he started speaking volubly, impatiently.

"What's he saying?"

"He admits he wasn't telling the truth at first. But now he wants to tell everything. He knows his own innocence is bound to be established. . . . When he came up on deck, the sailor was already making off. He followed, keeping his distance. The man led him along the Amsterdiep to the neighborhood of the Popingas' house, where he hid. Wondering what it was all about, Oosting hid in turn."

"And later he heard the shot fired?"

"Yes. . . . But he couldn't catch the man, who ran away."

"He saw him enter the house?"

"The garden, at any rate. . . . He thinks he must have climbed up to the second floor by means of the drainpipe."

Maigret smiled. The vague, happy smile of a man who has dined well and whose digestion is excellent.

"Would he recognize the man again?"

Translation. A shrug of the shoulders from the Baes.

"He's not sure."

"Did he see Barens spying on Beetje and Popinga?"

"Yes."

"And because he was afraid of being accused himself, he thought the best way to put the police on the right track was to get Barens to tell them?"

"Exactly. That's what he says. . . . But I ought not to believe him, ought I? . . . Of course he's guilty. I can see that now."

Duclos was fidgeting with impatience. Oosting, on the other hand, was perfectly calm, like a man who is prepared for the worst. He spoke again, and the Dutch detective promptly translated.

"He says we can do what we like with him now, but he wants us to know that Popinga was his friend and benefactor."

"What *are* you going to do with him?"

"I'll have to detain him. He admits he was there. . . ."

The effect of the brandy had not worn off. Pijpekamp's voice was louder than usual, his gestures jerky, his decisions abrupt. He wanted to appear to be a man who knew how to make up his mind. He was no longer the docile interpreter. Now that the solution to the case was obvious, he would show this foreigner how good the Dutch police were.

His face grew serious. He looked important. Once more he rang the bell.

When the policeman hurried in, he gave orders succinctly, at the same time tapping the table with a paper knife.

"Arrest this man. Lock him up. I'll see him again later."

The orders were given in Dutch, but there was no need for translation now.

With that he got up, saying:

"It won't be long before we have the whole thing cleared up. I will certainly mention the assistance you've given us. . . . Your countryman is free to go, and I greatly regret that his tour has been interrupted."

He spoke with the utmost self-assurance. It would have given him a shock to know what Maigret was thinking:

You're going to regret this, my friend! You're going to regret it bitterly, when you've had time to cool down!

Pijpekamp opened the door, but Maigret was in no hurry to take his leave.

"I'd like to ask you just one thing more," he began, in the sweetest of tones.

"Certainly, my dear fellow. What is it?"

"It's not yet four. . . . Perhaps this evening we might reconstruct the crime, with all the people present who were directly or indirectly mixed up in it. . . . You might jot down the names, please. . . . Madame Popinga, Any, Monsieur Duclos, Barens, the Wienands, Beetje, Oosting, and, last, Monsieur Liewens, Beetje's father."

"What do you want to do?"

"I want to go through the evening step by step, from the moment the professor finished his lecture at the Hotel Van Hasselt."

A pause. Pijpekamp was thinking it over.

"I must telephone Groningen," he said finally, "and ask whether it's all right. . . . But I'm afraid there'll be one person missing—Conrad Popinga."

Then, afraid the joke was in bad taste, he shot a furtive glance at the two Frenchmen. But Maigret took it quite seriously.

"Don't bother about that," he said. "I'll take Popinga's part myself."

Then, as he turned to go, he added:

"And many thanks for the excellent lunch."

— 8 —

Beetje and Her Father

Instead of going through the town from the police station to the Hotel Van Hasselt, Maigret went along the quay, accompanied by Jean Duclos, whose face and whole demeanor radiated bad temper.

"I suppose you know," he said at last, "that you're making yourself most objectionable?"

As he spoke his eyes were fixed on a crane, whose hoist swung only a foot or two above their heads.

"In what way?"

Duclos shrugged his shoulders and took several steps before answering.

"Is it possible you don't understand? . . . Perhaps you don't want to. . . . You're like all French people. . . ."

"I thought we were both French."

"With this difference, however: I have traveled widely. In fact, I think I could justifiably call myself a European, rather than a Frenchman. Wherever I go, I can fall into the ways of the country. While you . . .

you simply crash straight through everything regardless of the consequences, blind to everything that requires a little discrimination. . . ."

"Without stopping to wonder, for instance, whether or not it's desirable that the murderer be caught!"

"Why shouldn't you stop to wonder?" burst out the professor. "Why shouldn't you discriminate? . . . This isn't a dirty crime. It isn't the work of a professional killer, or any other sort of ordinary criminal. The question of robbery hasn't arisen. . . . In other words, the person who did it is not necessarily a danger to society."

"In which case . . . ?"

Maigret was smoking his pipe with obvious relish, striding along easily, his hands behind his back.

"You've only got to look around . . ." said Duclos, with a wave of his hand that embraced the whole scene: the tidy little town where everything was arranged as neatly as in a good housewife's cupboard; the harbor too small to have any of the sordidness that so often belongs to ports; happy, serene people clattering along in their varnished sabots.

Then he went on:

"Everyone earns his living. Everyone's more or less content. Everyone holds his instincts in check because his neighbor does the same, and that's the basis of all social life. . . . Pijpekamp will tell you that theft is a rare occurrence here—partly because when it does occur it's severely punished. For stealing a loaf of bread, you don't get off with less than a few weeks in prison. . . . Do you see any signs of disorder? . . . None. No tramps. No beggars. It's the very embodiment of cleanliness and order."

"And I've crashed in like a bull in a china shop! Is that it?"

"Look at those houses over there on the left, near the Amsterdiep. That's where the best people live. People of wealth, or at any rate of substance. People who have power or influence in the locality. Everybody knows them. They include the mayor, the clergy, teachers, and officials, all of whom make it their business to see that the town is kept quiet and peaceful, to see that everybody stays in his proper place without damaging his neighbor's interests. These people—as I've told you before—don't even allow themselves to enter a café for fear of setting a bad example. . . . And now a crime has been committed—and the moment you poke your nose in, you sniff some family scandal. . . ."

Maigret listened while looking at the boats, whose decks, because it was high tide, were well above the quay.

"I don't know what Pijpekamp thinks about it. He is a very respected man, by the way. All I know is that it would have been far better for everybody if it had been given out that Popinga had been killed by a foreign sailor, and that the police were pursuing their investigations. . . . Yes. Far better for everybody. Better for Madame Popinga. Better for her family, particularly for her father, who is a man of considerable repute in the intellectual world. Better for Beetje and for her father. Above all, better for the public welfare, for the people in all these other houses, who watch with respect all that goes on in the big houses by the Amsterdiep. Whatever is done over there, they want to do the same. . . . And you . . . you want truth for truth's sake—or for the personal satisfaction of unraveling your little mystery."

111

"You're putting it in your own words, Professor, but in substance what you say is what Pijpekamp said to you this morning. Isn't that so? . . . And he asked your advice as to the best method of dampening my unseemly zeal. . . . And you told him that in France people like me are disposed of with a hearty meal, even with a tip."

"We didn't go into details."

"Do you know what I think, Monsieur Duclos?"

Maigret had stopped and was looking at the harbor. A little bumboat, its motor making a noise like a fusillade, was going from ship to ship, selling bread, spices, tobacco, pipes, and schnapps.

"What?"

"I think you were lucky to have come out of the bathroom holding the revolver in your hand."

"What do you mean by that?"

"Nothing. . . . But I'd like you to assure me once more that you saw nobody in the bathroom."

"I saw nobody."

"And you heard nothing?"

Duclos looked away. Maigret repeated the question.

"I didn't hear anything definite. . . . It's only a vague impression, but there might have been a sound coming from under the lid over the tub."

"Excuse me, I must be off. . . . I think that's someone waiting for me."

Maigret strode off toward the entrance of the Hotel Van Hasselt. On the sidewalk in front, Beetje Liewens was walking up and down, obviously waiting for his return.

She tried to give him her usual smile, but without much success. She was obviously nervous, glancing up and down the street as though afraid of being seen.

"I've been waiting for you nearly half an hour."

"Won't you come in?"

"Not in the café. Could we go somewhere else?"

In the hallway Maigret hesitated. He couldn't very well take her up to his room. He pushed open the door of the long empty room used for dances and other festivities, the room where the professor's lecture had taken place the week before.

By the light of day it looked dusty and prosaic. The piano was open. A big drum stood in one corner. Chairs were stacked, one on top of the other, almost to the ceiling. The walls were still hung with paper garlands left from some dance.

Maigret ushered Beetje in and closed the door behind him. Their steps echoed in the emptiness. In spite of her nervousness, Beetje looked as seductive as ever in a blue tailored suit and white blouse.

"So you've managed to escape?"

She didn't answer at once. Evidently she had a lot to say and didn't know where to begin.

"Yes, I got out," she said at last. "I couldn't bear it any longer. I was afraid. The servant came and told me that my father was furious. She thought he was in such a state he might even kill me. . . . Last night we went into the house together without speaking. He led me to my room and locked the door without saying so much as a word. He's always like that when he's angry. . . . This afternoon the servant talked to me through the keyhole. She told me he had been out and come back about twelve o'clock, his face white. He had his lunch;

113

then he'd walked around the farm like a man possessed. Finally he went and visited my mother's grave. He always goes there when he has an important decision to make. . . .

"Then I got out by the window. . . . I don't want to go back. . . . I'm afraid to. . . . You don't know my father."

"One question . . ." interrupted Maigret.

He looked at the little kid bag she was holding.

"How much money did you bring away with you?"

"I don't know. . . . About five hundred florins."

"Which you had in your room?"

She blushed, stammering:

"They were in my bureau. . . . I thought of going to the station. But there's always a policeman there. . . . Then I thought of you."

They were standing much as they might have stood in a station waiting room. It was a place where ease and intimacy were impossible. They didn't even think of taking two chairs down from the stack.

If Beetje was nervous, she was nevertheless not the one to lose her head. Perhaps it was for that reason that Maigret looked at her with a certain hostility. It showed in his voice as he asked suddenly:

"How many men have you asked to elope with you?"

The question staggered her. She looked down, muttering:

"What?"

"First of all, Popinga. . . . Or was he the first?"

"I don't understand."

"I asked if he was the first."

A long pause. Then:

"I didn't think you'd be so horrid to me. . . . I came . . ."

"Was he the first? You've been with him for the last year, but before that?"

"I . . . I did flirt a little with the gymnastics teacher at the lycée in Groningen."

"Flirted?"

"It was he . . . he who . . ."

"Right! So he was your lover before Popinga came on the scene. Have you been anybody else's mistress as well?"

"Never!" she exclaimed indignantly.

"What about Cor?"

"Not with him. On my honor . . ."

"Yet you've been meeting him at night."

"Because he was in love with me. He had to pluck up all his courage to kiss me. There was nothing more to it than that."

"Nothing more? Just think! The last time you saw him—the time I interrupted you—weren't you asking him to run away with you?"

"How did you know?"

He almost burst out laughing. Her simplicity was really disarming. She was recovering her self-possession. She spoke of these matters with quite remarkable candor.

"What did he say to you? That he didn't want to?"

"He was frightened. He said he had no money."

"And you told him you would see to that. . . . For a long time now you've been thinking of how to get away. In fact, your whole aim in life is to leave Delfzijl

115

and see the world, and you don't care very much who you go with."

"I wouldn't go with *anyone*," she said snappily. "You're being horrid again. You don't want to understand me."

"Oh, yes, I do. But it doesn't require any great effort. You love life, and want to get the most out of it."

She looked down, fidgeting, at her bag.

"Your father's model farm bores you to distraction. That's not at all the life you've mapped out for yourself. But it's difficult to get away unless someone takes you. So you start scheming. First of all, the gymnastics teacher. But he wasn't playing. Back in Delfzijl you pick on Popinga as the most likely. He's not quite so sober-minded as the others. He's knocked about the world. He, too, loves life and finds the restrictions and prejudices of a provincial town irksome. So you cast your net. . . ."

"You have no right to say such things."

"Perhaps I exaggerate a little. I ought not to put *all* the responsibility on your shoulders. You're as pretty as the devil, and it may be that he responded up to a point. But I can't think he went very far; he was too frightened of complications, frightened of his wife, of Any, of his superior, perhaps even of his pupils."

"Of Any more than anyone."

"We'll come to her later. . . . As I said before, you cast your net. Not a day passes that you don't cross his path. You take fruit and homemade cakes—to his wife, of course. And before long it's an accepted thing that you pop in and out of the house almost like a member of the family. . . . And then you get him to see you home. . . . After a while you get on kissing terms. And a little later you're writing letters to him full of plans for your escape."

"Have you read them?"

"I know what's in some of them."

"And you're convinced that he didn't begin it?"

Her anger was rising.

"Right at the beginning, he told me he was unhappy, that Madame Popinga didn't understand him, and that all she thought about was what the neighbors would say. He said Delfzijl was a rotten hole, and that the life he was living wasn't life at all, and that . . ."

"Yes, yes, I know."

"So you see . . ."

"Sixty married men out of a hundred say all that to the first pretty young thing they meet. But Conrad Popinga had the misfortune to say it to a girl who took him at his word, and meant business."

"You're talking like a cad."

She stressed the word with a little stamp of her foot. She could have cried with vexation.

"Then at last, when he kept putting off the grand day of departure, you began to realize that it was never going to happen. . . ."

"It's not true."

"Oh, yes, it is! And it's proved by the fact that you were already putting a second iron in the fire. . . . If not Popinga, then Cor would have to do. With him, of course, you had to be wary. He's a shy, well-brought-up young man, and it wouldn't do to frighten him."

"You brute!"

"I don't think I'm far wrong, am I?"

"You hate me. I know you do."

"Good gracious, no. Not in the slightest."

"Yes, you do. You have no pity, and I'm so un-happy. . . . I loved Conrad. . . ."

"And Cor too? And the gymnastics teacher?"

Now she really did cry.

"I tell you . . ."

"That you loved them all! Perhaps you did, in your own way. You loved them because they represented escape to another life. Life in the great world, the life you've been dreaming about."

She was no longer listening. With a sigh she said:

"I shouldn't have come. . . . I thought . . ."

"That I would take you under my protection? . . . Isn't that just what I'm doing? . . . Only, I can't look upon you as anybody's victim, nor as a heroine. You're greedy for all the good things in life, and, beyond that, you're rather stupid, rather selfish. That's about all. There are plenty of others who are neither better nor worse than you are."

She looked at him with wet eyes in which there was actually a ray of hope.

"Everybody hates me," she groaned.

"Who do you mean by everybody?"

"Most of all Madame Popinga, because I'm not like her. She'd like me to spend all my days knitting for the poor, or making clothes for the natives of the South Sea Islands. I know she holds me up to other girls as an example, an example of what one should not be like! . . . In fact, she even said that I'd come to a bad end if I wasn't married soon. I know she did. They told me so."

Through her words, Maigret caught the stale per-fume of a provincial town. Sewing meetings. The young ladies of the best families gathered around the local lady bountiful. Whispered gossip. Heart-to-heart talks with an undercurrent of cattiness.

"Then there's Any. She's even worse. . . ."

"She hates you?"

"Yes. She even goes so far as to leave the room when I arrive. . . . I'm sure she guessed the truth long ago. . . . Madame Popinga is, after all, a good woman. If I couldn't stand her, it was because she wanted to make me over, dress soberly, and read dull books. But that doesn't change the fact that she's a good woman, far too good to be suspicious about her husband. . . . In fact, it was she who used to tell him to see me home."

A strange smile flitted across Maigret's face.

"Any's quite different. I don't need to tell you she's ugly, do I? You've seen her. With those teeth of hers, she never had a chance; and what's more, she knows it. . . . That's why she took up law—to have a profession. She pretends to be a man-hater and belongs to feminist groups and that kind of thing. . . ."

Beetje was working herself up again. This was obviously an old grudge.

"And she thought it was her business to keep an eye on Conrad. Since she has no choice but to remain virtuous herself, she takes it upon herself to see that others are. . . . You see what I mean?

"She guessed—I'm sure she did. And she wanted to get Conrad away from me. . . . Cor, too, for that matter . . . It didn't escape her notice that men were always looking at me. Even Wienand, who blushes every time I speak to him. And there's another who's got her knife into me—Madame Wienand. . . .

"Any may not have said anything about us to her

119

sister. But I think she did. In fact, I bet it was she who found my letters."

"Then perhaps it was Any who killed Conrad?" asked Maigret bluntly.

Beetje began to hedge at once.

"I didn't say that. I really don't know. All I know is that she's a snake in the grass. . . . Is it my fault that she's ugly?"

"Are you sure there's never been a man in her life?"

A smile, or, rather, a little laugh from Beetje. Such a laugh! The triumphant smirk of a girl who knows her charms and gloats over another's lack of them. Had Any a man in her life? She might have answered something tarter, but all she said was:

"Nobody around here, at any rate."

"Did she hate her brother-in-law too?"

"I don't know. Maybe not. Anyhow, that's different. He was one of the family, and so she could regard him as being partly her property. And she could easily persuade herself it was her duty to protect him from all temptations."

"But not kill him?"

"What are you thinking? Why are you always harping on that?"

"Don't bother about what I'm thinking. Just answer my questions. . . . But we'll let that go. Here's another one: Did Oosting know of your relations with Conrad?"

"What have they told you about that?"

"You used to go on their seal-shooting trips on the Workum sandbanks. And you used to sleep on board."

"Sometimes."

"And the Baes left you two to share the cabin?"

"It was quite natural. He preferred to sleep on deck, to be able to keep a lookout."

"Quite so. And have you seen him since . . . since the murder?"

"No. I can swear to that."

"Has he ever made a pass at you?"

A nervous titter.

"Him?"

Was she giggling with satisfaction? It didn't seem so. It was more as though she might cry again, with exasperation.

Madame Van Hasselt, who had heard voices, put her head around the door, but quickly withdrew, muttering excuses.

A pause. Then:

"Do you really think your father's capable of killing you?"

"Yes. I know he is."

"In that case, he was capable of killing Conrad for carrying on with you."

Her eyes opened wide. She looked scared.

"No," she protested. "It isn't true. It wasn't Papa."

"Yet when you arrived home on the night of the crime, he wasn't there."

"How do you know?"

"He got home a little after you, didn't he?"

"Right after . . . But . . ."

"In your last letters you seemed to be losing patience. You were beginning to realize that Conrad would slip through your fingers, that he was too frightened of his wife to run off with you, or perhaps he didn't really want to."

"What do you mean?"

"Nothing. I was just getting things clear in my mind.
. . . I don't suppose it'll be long before your father arrives."

She looked anxiously around, as though for a way
of escape.

"You needn't be afraid. I'll see that nothing hap-
pens to you. I need you tonight."

"Tonight?"

"Yes. We're going to reconstruct the crime, and I
want everybody to play his part."

"He'll kill me."

"Who will?"

"My father."

"I'll be there. You needn't worry."

"But . . ."

The door opened. Jean Duclos came in, shut it
quickly behind him, and turned the key in the lock. He
looked worried.

"Look out! Liewens is here. . . . He . . ."

"Take her upstairs to your room."

"To my . . . ?"

"To mine, if you'd rather."

Steps could be heard in the hallway. There was a
door at the other end of the room, leading to the ser-
vants' quarters and the back stairs. The two made a hasty
exit through it.

Maigret unlocked the door and found himself face
to face with the farmer. The latter, looking over the
inspector's shoulder, called:

"Beetje!"

Once more Maigret had the baffling experience of

having to deal with a man to whom he could not speak. All he could do was use his bulk to obstruct the way, thus giving the others time to make good their escape. He tried, however, not to do it too obviously; he didn't want to enrage the man.

A moment or two later Duclos came downstairs, trying, without much success, to look unconcerned.

"Tell him his daughter will be handed back to him tonight. And tell him that we'll need him, too, for the reconstruction of the crime."

"Must I?"

"Do what I tell you! *Sacrebleu!*"

Duclos translated in his most coaxing voice. The farmer looked from one to the other of them.

"Now tell him that this very evening the murderer will be under lock and key."

Again the professor translated. As the last word was pronounced, Maigret just had time to pounce on Liewens, who had whipped out a revolver and was lifting it toward his own temple.

The struggle was short. Maigret had sprung with all his weight and strength. In a second Liewens was on the floor, the revolver wrenched out of his grasp, while the pile of chairs they had bumped into came hurtling down with a crash, the leg of one scratching Maigret's forehead on its way.

"Lock the door," shouted Maigret to Duclos. "We don't need any spectators."

He rose to his feet, panting.

− 9 −

A Dreary Gathering

It was exactly seven-thirty. The Wienands were the first to arrive. In the dance-and-lecture room of the Hotel Van Hasselt they found three men waiting, each standing by himself in silent preoccupation. Jean Duclos was walking nervously up and down from one end of the room to the other; Liewens was sitting on a chair, a glum, set look on his face; Maigret, his pipe between his teeth, was leaning against the piano.

A single lamp, high overhead, shed a bleak inadequate light, but no one seemed to think of switching on the others. The chairs were stacked again at the end of the room, except for the few that Maigret had taken and set in a row, to represent the front row of seats at the lecture.

On the empty platform were a chair and a table covered by a green cloth.

The Wienands, in their Sunday best, had carried out their instructions to the letter, bringing their two children with them. It wasn't difficult to guess that they had rushed away from a hasty meal, leaving their dining room in disorder.

Monsieur Wienand had taken off his hat as he came into the room, and he looked around for someone to speak to. He made a move toward the professor, but thought better of it. Finally he drew his family into a corner, where they stood in silence. His collar was too high, his tie crooked.

Cornélius Barens was next, pale and fidgety, looking as though the least thing would send him fleeing for his life. He, too, like Wienand, wanted to find somebody to speak to, but no one gave him the least encouragement, and he edged away to the back of the room and leaned against the stack of chairs.

Oosting, led in by Pijpekamp, gave Maigret a serious, searching look. Behind him came Madame Popinga, then Any, who walked in briskly, stopped for a second, and then went straight toward the row of chairs.

Maigret turned to Pijpekamp:

"You can bring down Beetje. Get one of your men to watch Liewens and Oosting. They weren't here on the night of the crime, and we won't be wanting them until later. They'd better sit right at the back."

Beetje entered the room shyly, looking thoroughly uncomfortable, but the sight of Any and Madame Popinga was enough to pull her together. Her whole body stiffened, and she gave a little toss of her head.

No one spoke. In fact, it hardly seemed as though anyone was breathing. Not that the atmosphere was in any way tense or dramatic. It wasn't. To say it was mean would be nearer the mark.

A pathetic handful of people in that big room, silent under the bleak light that hardly reached into the corners.

It required quite an effort to realize that, only a few days before, all the notables of Delfzijl had been there. They had paid for the right to sit in those chairs that were now stacked at the end of the room. In their best clothes, they had sailed in, playing to the gallery, smiling, bowing, shaking hands, taking their seats, and then clapping heartily as Jean Duclos appeared on the platform.

Tonight it was as if the same scene was being viewed through the wrong end of the telescope.

Everybody waited. No one had the least idea what was going to happen. Yet for the most part it was not anxiety and pain that were written on their faces. Just gloomy looks, bereft of any sparkle. Features drawn, not by emotion, but by lassitude. And the light made everyone's complexion gray. Even Beetje looked dull and plain.

There was nothing impressive about these proceedings, nor anything comic. Simply a wretched, halfhearted rehearsal by a rotten company!

Outside, people gathered in silent groups. By the end of the afternoon, the news had reached almost everyone in the town that something was going to happen at the Hotel Van Hasselt. Certainly none of them imagined that the spectacle inside was so unromantic.

At last Maigret moved, turning to Madame Popinga.

"Will you sit in the same seat you had the other night?"

A few hours before, her nerves had been strung to tragic pitch. There was nothing left of that now. She looked older. Her coat was so badly made that one shoulder looked broader than the other, and one couldn't help noticing her big feet and the scar on her neck below the ear.

Any cut a still poorer figure. Her features had never looked so irregular. Her clothes were absurd, and there was something niggardly about them.

Madame Popinga took her place in the middle of the front row, the place of honor. The last time she had sat there, with all Delfzijl behind her, she had been pink with pride.

"Who sat beside you?"

"The captain of the training ship."

"And on the other side?"

"Monsieur Wienand."

The latter was requested to take his place. He still had his coat on, and sat down awkwardly, trying not to catch anybody's eye.

"And Madame Wienand?"

"At the end of the row, because of the children."

"Beetje?"

The girl took her seat before Madame Popinga could answer. She was two seats from Any, the chair between them being the one Conrad Popinga had sat in.

Pijpekamp, standing in the back, was uneasy, altogether out of his depth. Duclos was dejectedly waiting to be called upon to play his part.

"Go up on the platform," said Maigret.

Of all the people in the room, he was perhaps the most pitiable. Standing on the platform, thin, badly dressed, listless, it was impossible to imagine him having been the great attraction a week earlier.

Another pause. The silence was as bleak as that miserable light falling from the high ceiling. Four or five times Oosting coughed at the back of the room.

Even Maigret could hardly have been called comfortable. He looked mournfully at the spurious drama he was staging, his eyes resting on one character after the other, taking in the smallest details—the way Beetje sat in her chair, Any's skirt, which was too long, the professor's dirty fingernails as he stood drumming on the table, trying not to look too silly.

"How long did you speak?"

"Three-quarters of an hour."

"Did you read the lecture?"

"Certainly not. This was the twentieth time I'd given it. I didn't once have to glance at my notes."

"So you were looking at your audience."

Maigret sat down for a moment between Any and Beetje. The chairs were close together, and he was literally wedged between them, his knee pressing against Beetje's.

"What time did the lecture finish?"

"Just before nine. We began with some music."

The piano was still open, a Chopin polonaise still on it. Madame Popinga was chewing the corner of her handkerchief. Oosting shuffled his feet at the back of the room. Maigret left his chair and started walking around.

"Monsieur Duclos, will you kindly run through the principal points of your lecture?"

But Duclos was incapable of that, incapable of doing what he was asked. He hesitated, coughed, and began, word for word, from the beginning:

"I will not insult the intelligent audience I have before me tonight by . . ."

"Excuse me! You were speaking, I think, of crime. What was the exact subject?"

"The responsibility of criminals for their actions."

"And you were maintaining . . . ?"

"That it is really society itself which is responsible for all the faults of its members, including those faults that go by the name of crime. . . . Life is organized for the best possible welfare of everybody. . . . We have created social classes, and it is essential that every individual should be properly brought up to take his place in one of them. . . ."

He stared at the green cloth covering the table as he spoke. His voice was faint and lacked all authority.

"That's enough," groaned Maigret. "I know that story: 'There are some individuals who for one reason or another cannot be fit into any social class. They are fundamentally unadaptable, or, if you prefer it, diseased. It is they who provide what we call criminals and must therefore be placed in a class of their own.' . . . Something of that sort, wasn't it? We've heard it many times before. . . . Conclusion: 'Do away with prisons and build more hospitals.'"

The professor's only answer was a sulky look.

"So you spoke in that vein for three-quarters of an hour, illustrating your points with striking examples. You quoted Lombroso and a host of others, finishing with Freud."

He looked at his watch and, speaking to the row of seated people who represented the audience, said:

"I must ask you to wait just a few minutes more."

The moment was chosen by one of the children to set up a howl. Her mother, whose nerves were stretched, shook her to make her keep quiet. When that didn't

129

work, her father took her on his knee and tried coaxing. That didn't work either, so he pinched her arm.

You had to look at the empty chair between Any and Beetje to realize that, after all, something serious was going on. But, even so, wasn't it all rather unremarkable? Was Beetje, with her healthy but insipidly pretty face, worth all the trouble she had caused?

The feeble light had the virtue of showing up the naked truth by destroying all the glow and glamour that generally concealed it. It did its work effectively with Beetje. Insipidly pretty, was she? Hardly that. What had she, then, that entitled her to play a star's part in the drama? To put it crudely, she had two things, and two things only: two fine round buxom breasts that were sufficiently outlined by her silk blouse to make them all the more alluring. Eighteen-year-old breasts, which the slightest quiver made to seem palpitating with life.

Beyond her, Madame Popinga, who neither now nor at eighteen ever had such breasts as those. Madame Popinga dressed in layer upon layer of sober clothing, which was not in bad taste, but in no taste at all.

And Any, angular, ugly, flat-chested, whose only piquancy lay in being enigmatic.

Popinga had had the bad luck to cross Beetje's path, Popinga the bon vivant, a seafaring man who'd come home to roost too soon, who still had a sweet tooth for the world's more sensuous pleasures. Had he ever really looked at Beetje's face and her glassy, china-blue eyes? If he had, he had certainly not seen behind them, seen the grappling iron she had ready to hook on to any man who could take her off somewhere—anywhere that wasn't Delfzijl.

130

He had merely glanced at the rest of her. All his eyes had really rested on was that young, seductive, supple body. . . .

As for Madame Wienand, she could hardly be called a woman at all. Mother, housewife, she was now blowing the nose of her little girl, whose tears were gradually petering out.

"Do you want me to stay here?" asked Duclos from the platform.

"Please."

Maigret walked back to Pijpekamp and whispered a few words in his ear. The Groningen detective left a moment later with Oosting.

In another room people were playing billiards, and every few seconds the clack of ivory balls could be heard.

In the lecture room the atmosphere was now thoroughly oppressive. It was something like a spiritualist séance. Everybody expected something uncanny to happen. Everybody was cowed, except Any, who suddenly got up and, after a considerable effort to find her voice, said:

"I can't see what all this is leading to. It's . . . it's . . ."

"It's time," cut in Maigret shortly. "Where's Cornélius?"

He had forgotten all about him. He found him far from the others, his back to the wall.

"Why didn't you take your proper place?"

"You said we were to be where we were the other evening . . ."

His eyes darted here and there nervously. The words came jerkily.

131

"And the other evening I was with my shipmates in the fifty-cent seats."

Maigret took no further notice of him, but went and opened a door that led through a porch directly to the street and enabled people to come and go without passing through the café. He glanced outside. The people who had been gathered there seemed, for the most part, to have dispersed. There were only three or four silhouettes visible in the darkness.

Turning back to the room, he said:

"I suppose that, as soon as the lecture was over, people crowded around the platform to congratulate the speaker. . . ."

No one answered, but the words sufficed to recall the scene. A general bustle, the scrape of chairs on the floor, the bulk of the audience streaming slowly through the exit, while the more important people gathered at the platform to shake the professor's hand and compliment him on his success. The room slowly emptying. The last group finally moving toward the door. . . . Cornélius joining the Popingas. . . .

"You can step down now, Monsieur Duclos."

Everyone rose, but then stood still, uncertain of what was expected of them. All eyes were on Maigret. Any and Beetje, though standing almost shoulder to shoulder, ignored each other's presence. Wienand carried the youngest of the children.

"This way, please."

As they started toward the door, he said:

"We're going to walk to the house in the same order as last week. . . . Madame Popinga and Monsieur Duclos . . ."

They looked awkwardly at each other, hesitated, then went through the door together and out into the darkness.

"Next, Mademoiselle Beetje. You were walking with Popinga. You follow the others. I'll be joining you in a moment."

She didn't like walking alone. She was still frightened of her father, though he was in a far corner of the room with a policeman standing next to him.

"Monsieur and Madame Wienand . . ."

They stepped off with less embarrassment than the others. Having the children to look after made it easier.

"Mademoiselle Any and Cornélius . . ."

The latter almost broke down. Biting his lip, however, he pulled himself together, passed Maigret, and went out with Any.

The inspector then turned to the policeman standing by Liewens.

"At this time, on the night of the crime, he was at home. . . ."

But the policeman looked at him blankly, and he had to call Duclos back to act as interpreter.

"Tell him to take Liewens to the farm, and make him do exactly what he did before."

Having said that, Maigret sent the professor back to his place in the procession. If there had been a hearse in front, it would have been rather like a funeral procession—one, however, that was going badly. There were halts and hesitations, and the leading pair kept glancing around to make sure they were being followed.

Madame Van Hasselt, standing in the hotel entrance, watched them pass by without once stopping her conversation with the billiard players.

All the shops were shut; in fact, three-quarters of the town was already in bed and asleep. Madame Popinga and the professor led the way along the quay. Duclos was talking, and it wasn't hard to guess that he was trying to reassure his companion.

There were alternations of light and darkness, since the lampposts were too far apart for one circle of light to reach to the next. The black water was just visible, and the dark hulls of the boats. Beetje, with Any behind her, tried to walk with easy grace. But walking alone made her self-conscious.

Several yards separated each couple. A little farther on, Oosting's boat was clearly visible. It was easy to distinguish, being the only one painted white. No light came through the portholes. The quay was deserted.

"Will you all stop, please, exactly where you are?" Maigret called out, loud enough to be heard by everybody.

They stood stiffly where they were. The beam of light from the lighthouse swept by over their heads without touching them.

Maigret spoke to Any.

"Were you in exactly the same place in the column the other night?"

"Yes."

"And you, Cornélius?"

"Yes . . . at least, I think so. . . ."

"Are you sure of it? You were walking side by side with Mademoiselle Any?"

"Yes. That is, up to this point. About ten yards far-

134

ther on, Any pointed out that one of the children's coats was trailing on the ground."

"And you ran forward to the Wienands and let them know?"

"I told Madame Wienand."

"It took only a few seconds, I suppose?"

"Yes. Then the Wienands went on, while I waited for Any."

"You didn't notice anything peculiar?"

"Nothing."

"Will everyone please take ten steps forward," ordered Maigret, and then:

"Another five, please."

This brought Any exactly abreast of Oosting's boat.

"Now go up to the Wienands, Cornélius. . . ."

And to Any:

"Take that cap lying on the cabin roof."

To do so, she had to take only three steps and then one to the deck, from which position it was within easy reach. It was clearly visible, a dark thing against a light background. A metallic glint even showed the position of its badge.

"Why do you ask me to do that?"

"Go on! Take it!"

They were not speaking loudly, and the people in front were straining their ears, wondering what was going on.

"But I didn't . . ."

"No matter whether you did or you didn't. There's one person missing tonight, and it may be that others have to play his part. . . . Don't forget this is only an experiment."

She took the cap without another word.

"Hide it under your coat."

Maigret himself jumped on board and called out:

"Pijpekamp."

"*Ya.*"

The detective's head emerged from the cabin. Standing inside, his head just under the coach roof, he had been able to see everything through one of the portholes in the coaming. He came on deck, the Baes following.

"Did you see?" asked Maigret.

Pijpekamp nodded.

"Good. Now take Oosting off, where he went the other night. . . . Any! Overtake Cornélius, will you? And will everybody please go on toward the house."

Maigret stepped back to the quay.

"I'm taking Popinga's place."

Hurrying forward, he joined the procession by Beetje's side. In front were Madame Popinga and Duclos, behind were the Wienands, followed by Any and Cornélius. From behind them all came the sound of steps: Oosting and Pijpekamp, bringing up the rear, though keeping their distance.

The last lampposts were left behind, and from now on the walk was in darkness—skirting the harbor, passing the lock gate that separated sea and canal, then on to the towpath, flanked by trees, with the Popingas' house five hundred yards ahead.

Beetje murmured:

"I can't understand what . . ."

"Not so loud. It's a calm night, and the people in front and behind can hear us as easily as we can hear

136

them. . . . And it was calm the other night. . . . So Popinga would be speaking to you in his ordinary voice, talking about everyday matters, perhaps discussing the lecture?"

"Yes."

"At the same time, you were whispering reproaches!"

"How did you know?"

"Never mind . . . Now for another question. Sitting next to him during the lecture, you wanted to hold his hand—and he repulsed you, didn't he?"

"Yes, he did at first."

"But you persisted?"

"Yes . . . It was perfectly safe, and he never used to be so cautious. Even in his own house he used to kiss me as soon as we were alone. Once, we were talking to Madame Popinga from the living room to the dining room, where she was putting things away—and all through the conversation he had me in his arms. But lately he was always telling me to be careful. . . ."

"So, while he made a show of talking about the lecture, you were throwing him reproaches under your breath? And you tried once more to persuade him to run away with you. . . ."

The night was indeed still. Steps rang out clearly in front and behind, and Maigret could even hear an occasional snatch of what Duclos was saying.

"I can assure you this has nothing whatever to do with any real police methods. . . ."

Behind the professor, Madame Wienand was scolding a child in Dutch.

Suddenly the Popingas' house emerged from the

137

darkness. There was no sign of any light. Madame Popinga stopped on the doorstep.

"You stopped like that, didn't you, because your husband had the key?"

"Yes."

"Your servant was in bed?"

"Yes . . . The same as today."

The successive couples had by this time been telescoped into a single group.

"Open the door, will you?" said Maigret.

She opened the door and switched on the light, which showed the hallway and the bamboo hatstand on the left.

"From now on, Popinga was in very high spirits, wasn't he?"

"Very. But it didn't seem altogether natural. Just a trifle forced."

Hats and coats were being removed and hung up in the hall.

"Just a moment! Did everybody take their things off here?"

"All except Any and me," said Madame Popinga. "We went up to our rooms to tidy ourselves."

"You went straight up? Who switched on the light in the living room?"

"It must have been Conrad."

"Go upstairs then, will you?"

He followed them up.

"Any had to go through your room to get to hers. Did she stop on the way?"

"No. I think she went straight through."

"Take off your things, just as you did last week. . . .

138

Leave your things in your own room, Mademoiselle Any, and the cap too. . . . What did you do next?"

Madame Popinga's lower lip quivered.

"A little dab of powder," she said. "And I hastily brushed my hair. . . . But I . . . I can hardly stand it. . . . It's dreadful. I have the feeling I can hear him now. Downstairs. Talking about the radio. Trying to get Radio Paris."

Madame Popinga threw her coat on her bed. She was weeping, though without tears. Any stood stiffly, right in the middle of Conrad's study, which was still serving as her bedroom.

"You went down together?"

"Yes . . . Or, no . . . I can't remember. I think Any came down a little later. I hurried to see to the guests."

"In that case, will you please go down now?"

He remained alone with Any. Without saying a word, he took the cap out of her hand, looked around the room, and finally hid it under the divan.

"Come."

"Do you really think . . . ?"

"No. Come. . . . Did you powder your face too?"

"Never!"

There were dark rings under her eyes. Maigret led her out of the room. The stairs creaked. Not a sound came from below. When they entered the living room the whole scene looked quite unreal—more like an exhibition of waxworks. No one had dared sit down. Madame Wienand, who was fussing with the children's ruffled hair, was apparently the only one who had dared to move at all.

"Take your places, please. The same places . . . Where's the radio?"

He found it himself before anyone answered. He switched it on and, turning the knobs, suddenly filled the room with alternate whistlings, cracklings, bursts of voices, and snatches of music. Finally he left it on a station that was broadcasting a recorded music-hall act in French.

"Le colon disait au capiston . . ."

Again there were cracklings. Maigret adjusted one of the knobs. Suddenly the voice came twice as loud as before:

". . . et c'est un bon type le capiston. . . . Mais le colon, mon vieux . . ."

The thick, sonorous voice resounded in the neat living room in which everyone stood as though turned to stone.

"Sit down!" thundered Maigret through the din. "Sit down and talk. What about the tea?"

He tried to look through the window, but the shutters were closed. Going to the front door, he opened it and called:

"Pijpekamp!"

"Yes," answered a voice from the darkness.

"Is he there?"

"Yes. Behind the second tree."

Maigret came back into the room. The front door slammed behind him. The music-hall act was finished and the announcer was saying:

"Disque Odéon numéro vingt-huit mille six cent soixante-quinze."

More cracklings; then jazz. Madame Popinga flattened herself against the wall. There was interference from another station, and under the jazz a nasal voice could just be made out, whining in some foreign language. Sometimes there was a whole series of splutterings, after which the music could be heard again.

Maigret looked for Beetje. She had collapsed into an armchair. Hot tears ran down her cheeks, and between her sobs she stammered:

"Conrad! . . . Poor Conrad! . . ."

Cornélius, looking like death, was biting his lip.

"What about the tea?" Maigret asked again.

"Not yet," answered Any. "First, they rolled back the carpet. They started dancing."

Beetje was shaken by a more violent sob. Maigret looked at the carpet, at the oak table with its embroidered cloth, at the window, at Madame Wienand, still preoccupied with her children. . . .

– 10 –

The Evening Drags On

Maigret's bulky figure as he leaned against the door seemed altogether too big for the small room. His face was gray, though not stern; in fact, his humanity had never been more obvious than when he spoke, slowly, quietly, in an almost muffled voice:

"The music goes on. . . . Barens helps Popinga roll up the carpet. In the corner there, Duclos holds forth to Madame Popinga and her sister. . . . Wienand and his wife hold a whispered consultation about whether they ought to be going, because it's getting late for the children. . . . Popinga has drunk a glass of brandy, and that's enough to get him going. He laughs. He hums to the music. He goes up to Beetje and asks her to dance with him. . . ."

Madame Popinga stared at the floor. Any's feverish pupils never left Maigret as he pursued his monologue.

"The murderer already knows what he's going to do. . . . There's someone in this room who watches Conrad dancing, knowing that within a couple of hours this man who laughs a little too boisterously, not yet resigned to a quiet life, and still trying desperately to have a good time in spite of everything—that this man will be lying dead. . . ."

His words sent a shock through the little audience. Madame Popinga's mouth opened for a scream, which, however, remained under control. Beetje's sobs continued.

In a flash the atmosphere had changed. It was as though Conrad was there in the flesh. Conrad dancing, dancing with two eyes fixed upon him, the eyes that knew he would soon be dead.

Duclos was the only one who tried to make light of it.

"Very clever!" he scoffed.

Nobody appeared to have heard him, and his words were, in any case, half drowned by the music. But he persisted:

"I see now what you're driving at. An old trick. Play on the murderer's nerves by bringing him back into the atmosphere of his crime. Get him thoroughly scared, in the hope that he will be so obliging as to give himself away."

His sneering came faintly through the jazz. But no one was interested any longer in what the professor thought.

Madame Wienand whispered something in her husband's ear, and he rose timidly from his seat. He was going to speak, but Maigret saved him the trouble.

"Yes. That's all right. You can go."

Poor Madame Wienand, so respectable, so well brought up. She wanted to take her leave properly and

143

have the children say good night as good little children should. But the circumstances were too much for her. All she could do was silently give Madame Popinga a limp handshake, gather her brood, and make an ignominious exit.

The clock on the mantelpiece showed five past ten.

"Isn't it time for the tea yet?" asked Maigret.

"Yes," answered Any, getting up and going to the kitchen.

"Excuse me, Madame Popinga, but didn't you go to help her?"

"A little later."

"You found her in the kitchen?"

Madame Popinga passed her hand across her forehead. She was making a great effort to concentrate. She gazed hopelessly at the radio.

"I . . . I really can't say. Not for sure. At least . . . Wait a moment! I think she was coming out of the dining room. She'd been to get the sugar from the sideboard."

"Was the dining-room light on?"

"No . . . It might have been, but I don't think so."

"Did you speak to her?"

"Yes. Though that might have been in the kitchen. I remember saying, 'I hope Conrad won't drink any more, or he'll be overstepping the mark.' "

Maigret went into the hallway just as the front door closed behind the Wienands. The kitchen was brightly lit and spotlessly clean. The water was boiling on a gas ring. Any was in the act of taking the lid off the teapot.

"Don't bother to make any tea."

Any looked Maigret in the eye. They were alone.

"Why did you make me take the cap?" she asked.

"It doesn't matter. . . . Come . . ."

In the living room, again no one was speaking or moving.

"Have we got to listen to this music all night?" asked Duclos, feeling he must make a protest.

"Perhaps . . . There's someone else I'd like to see, and that's the maid."

Madame Popinga looked at Any, who answered:

"She's in bed. . . . She always goes to bed at nine."

"I see. Well, go and tell her to come down for a moment. . . . She needn't bother to dress."

In the same quiet, monotonous voice as before, he continued:

"You were dancing with Conrad, Beetje. . . . In the corner, they were talking seriously. . . . And someone knew there was going to be a murder. Someone knew that it was Popinga's last evening on this earth. . . ."

Noises overhead. Steps, the shutting of a door on the third floor, which was mostly garrets. Then more steps and a murmur of voices. Finally Any came back into the room; the maid hovered in the hallway.

"Come inside," growled Maigret. "Someone tell her to come in and not to be frightened."

She had a large flat face with ill-defined features. Though still bleary-eyed with sleep, she looked scared out of her wits. Over her cream-colored flannelette nightgown, which reached to her feet, she had merely slipped on her coat. Her hair was tousled.

Maigret once more enlisted the professor's services as interpreter.

"Ask her whether she was Popinga's mistress."

With a pained expression, Madame Popinga turned her head away. The question was translated. The girl shook her head.

"Ask her again. . . . No! Ask her if her master ever tried to get her consent."

Another vigorous denial.

"Tell her that she can be sent to prison if she doesn't tell the truth. . . . Let's get down to details. Did he ever kiss her? Did he ever go into her room when she was there?"

The answer this time was a sudden gush of tears.

"I never did anything wrong," pleaded the girl. "I never did. . . . I swear . . ."

Little as Duclos liked the job, he translated what she said. With her lips pursed, Any stared at the maid.

"Now go back to the first question: Was she his mistress?"

But the girl could no longer speak coherently. She wept, she wailed, she protested. She tried to explain and asked forgiveness.

"I don't think she was," said the professor at last. "When he was alone in the house with her, he'd fool around with her in the kitchen—put his arm around her waist, kiss her, that sort of thing. Once, he came into her room when she was dressing. He used to give her chocolate surreptitiously. . . . But, as far as I can make out, it went no farther than that."

"She can go back to bed."

They listened to the girl's retreating footsteps as she climbed the stairs. Instead of their ceasing when she

146

reached the third floor, there was the noise of her walking back and forth in her room, apparently moving things.

Turning to Any, Maigret said:

"Will you kindly go and see what she's doing?"

It wasn't long before Any reported:

"She says she's leaving the house at once. She won't stay a minute longer, because she could never look my sister in the face again. She'll go to Groningen, or somewhere, and never come back to Delfzijl again."

And, in an aggrieved tone, Any added:

"I suppose that's what you wanted!"

The evening was dragging on. It was getting late. A voice from the radio announced the end of the program:

"Notre audition est terminée. Bonsoir, mesdames; bonsoir, mesdemoiselles; bonsoir, messieurs."

Sudden silence. Then, dimly through the silence, faint music from another station. Suddenly it grew louder.

With a curt movement Maigret switched it off, and the silence was now complete, an almost piercing silence. Beetje was no longer sobbing, but her face was still buried in her hands.

"I suppose the conversation went on?" asked Maigret, his voice sounding tired.

No one answered. Every face showed the strain.

"I must apologize for this painful evening," said Maigret, turning toward Madame Popinga. "But don't forget that your husband was still alive. . . . He was here in this room talking and laughing. . . . Perhaps he'd had a second glass of brandy?"

"Yes."

147

"And he was a condemned man. Do you understand that? . . . Condemned by someone watching him
. . . And others who are here at this moment are holding back what they know, and are thus making themselves accomplices."

Cor hiccupped. He was still trembling.

"Isn't that so, Cornélius?" said Maigret to him point-
blank.

"No! . . . No! . . . It isn't true."

"Then what are you trembling for?"

"I . . . I . . ."

He was on the point of breaking down again, as he
had on the way back from the farm.

"Listen to me! We'll soon have reached the time when
Beetje left, escorted by Popinga. You left immediately
after, Cornélius. You followed them for a moment . . .
and you saw something. . . ."

"No! . . . It isn't true."

"We'll see about that. . . . After those three had
gone, the only people left were Madame Popinga, Mademoiselle Any, and Professor Duclos. They went upstairs."

Any nodded.

"Each of you went to his own room, didn't you?"

Then, once more rounding on Cor:

"Tell me what you saw."

The boy squirmed and wriggled. But he couldn't
escape from the grip of Maigret's stare.

"No! . . . Nothing! . . . Nothing!"

"You didn't see Oosting hidden behind a tree?"

"No."

"Yet you couldn't tear yourself away from the place.
. . . That means you saw something."

"I don't know. . . . I won't . . . No. It's not possible. . . ."

Everyone looked at him, but he avoided catching anybody's eye. And Maigret went on pitilessly:

"First of all you saw something on the towpath. The two bicycles were out of sight, but you knew they'd have to pass through the patch lit by the beam from the lighthouse. You were jealous. You waited. And you had a long time to wait. A time that didn't correspond to the distance they had to go."

"Yes."

"In other words, they'd stopped somewhere under the shadow of some lumber. . . . But that wasn't enough to frighten you. It might have angered you or plunged you in despair. But you saw something else, which alarmed you so much that you stayed where you were, instead of going back to the training ship. You were over by the lumberyard. There was only one window you could see from there. . . ."

It was those last words that unnerved the boy. He looked wildly around. Would he have the strength of mind to hold out?

"It isn't possible. You couldn't know that. I . . . I . . ."

"There was only one window you could see from there. Madame Popinga's . . . Someone was at that window. Someone who, like you, saw the couple take much too long to pass into the lighthouse beam. Someone who knew that Conrad and Beetje had stopped on the way."

"I was at the window," said Madame Popinga firmly.

Now it was Beetje's turn to look around wildly with frightened eyes.

149

To everyone's surprise, Maigret asked no further questions. Not that that brought any relief; it only added to the prevailing uneasiness. They seemed to have come to the climax, and the sudden pause only heightened the suspense.

The inspector went out into the hallway, opened the front door, and called out:

"Pijpekamp! Would you come here, please? Leave Oosting where he is."

Then, as the Dutchman approached:

"You saw the lights go on in the Wienands'? . . . I suppose they're off now?"

"Yes. They've gone to bed."

"And Oosting?"

"He's standing behind the tree."

The Groningen detective looked at everyone with surprise. They were all calm now, unbelievably calm, but they all looked as though they hadn't slept for nights and nights.

"Have you got the revolver?"

"Here it is."

Maigret took it and held it out to Duclos.

"Will you please go and put this in the place where you found it after the murder?"

There was no resistance left in the professor, and he meekly obeyed, rejoining them a moment later.

"Will you wait here a moment?" said Maigret to Pijpekamp. "I'm going out with Beetje Liewens, just as Popinga did. Madame Popinga will go up to her room. So will her sister and the professor. . . . I

150

want them to go through the same actions as on that night."

Then, turning to Beetje:

"Will you come?"

It was cold outside. Maigret led the girl to the shed at the back of the house, where he found Popinga's and two women's bicycles.

"Take one of those."

They cycled off in the direction of the lumberyard.

"Which of you suggested stopping?"

"Conrad."

"Was he still in high spirits?"

"No. As soon as we were alone together, he seemed to droop."

They were passing the stacks of lumber.

"We'll stop here. . . . Did he make love to you?"

"Yes, and no. That is, halfheartedly. He was definitely depressed by that time. Maybe it was the brandy. It made him lighthearted at first, then left him flat as a pancake. He put his arm around me. We were standing right here. . . . He told me he was very unhappy and that I was a real good sort. . . . Yes, he did. Those were his very words . . . that I was a real good sort, but that I'd come into his life too late. Then he went on to say that we had to be careful, or something dreadful might happen."

"What had you done with the bicycles?"

"We'd leaned them against the lumber. . . . His voice was tearful. He got like that sometimes when he drank. . . . He began saying that it wasn't on his account at all—that his life didn't matter—but it would be criminal at my age to ruin my life by plunging into a risky

151

adventure. . . . He swore he loved me, but that he couldn't bring himself to ruin my life. He told me that Cor was a nice boy, and I'd be happy with him when I once settled down. . . ."

"And then?"

She was breathing hard, obviously agitated. She burst out:

"I told him he was a coward. I tried to get on my bicycle."

"Did he stop you?"

"Yes. He seized the handlebar and wouldn't let go. He said:

" 'Let me explain. . . . I'm only thinking of you. It's . . .' "

"What did he explain?"

"Nothing. I didn't give him a chance. I threatened to shout if he didn't let go. He did, and I jumped on and pedaled off as hard as I could. He followed, talking all the time. But he couldn't catch up with me, and all I heard was:

" 'Beetje! Beetje! Do listen.' "

"Is that all?"

"When he saw that I'd reached the farm gate, he turned around. . . . I looked back at him and saw him riding off. He seemed to be hunched over his handlebar. . . . I thought he looked miserable."

"And you jumped on your bicycle again and rode after him?"

"No. I was too angry with him for trying to throw me into Cor's arms. I could see why. He wanted to be left in peace. . . . It was only when I reached the front door that I noticed I'd dropped my scarf. I was afraid

152

it might be found by the lumber stack, so I went back to look for it. . . . I didn't see anybody. But I was surprised, when I finally got home, to find that my father was still out. He came back a little later. He was pale, and there was a hard look in his eyes. He didn't say good night to me, and I guessed he'd been watching us. He could easily have been hiding in the lumberyard too.

"The next day he must have searched my room and found Conrad's letters, because I discovered they were missing. Then—well, you know the rest."

"Come along."

"Where?"

Maigret didn't bother to answer, and they bicycled back in silence to the Popingas' house. There was a light in Madame Popinga's window, but there was no sign of her.

"Do you really think she did it?"

But the inspector was thinking of Popinga.

He had retraced his steps, upset by the scene he had come from. Jumping off his bicycle, he had wheeled it around to the back. . . . He was tempted by Beetje, but incapable of taking the plunge.

Maigret got off, saying:

"Stay there, Beetje."

He wheeled his bicycle down the path that ran along the side of the house, and crossed the yard to the shed.

Duclos's window was lighted, and it was just possible to make out his figure sitting at the little table. Two yards farther on was the bathroom window, slightly open, but showing no light.

I don't suppose he was in any hurry to go in, thought

153

Maigret, his mind going back once more to Popinga. He bent his head just as I am doing as he wheeled his bicycle in under the roof.

Was he deliberately dawdling? He seemed to be waiting for something to happen. And, as a matter of fact, something did happen.

A little noise above, coming from the bathroom window, a metallic sound, the click of an unloaded revolver.

It was immediately followed by a scuffle . . . the thud of a body, perhaps two bodies, falling to the floor.

Maigret nipped into the house through the kitchen door and, dashing upstairs, switched on the bathroom light.

On the floor two men were wrestling. One of them was Pijpekamp, the other Cornélius Barens. As Maigret entered the room, the boy went limp, and his hand dropped a revolver.

It was the revolver Duclos had been told to replace on the bathroom windowsill, the revolver that had killed Conrad.

–11–

The Unwanted Solution

"Fool! . . ."

With that one word, Maigret grasped the boy by the collar and literally picked him up from the floor, holding him for a moment, because if he'd let go, the limp body would merely have sunk down again. Doors were opening, steps approaching.

"Everybody in the living room!" roared Maigret.

He picked up the revolver too. He didn't need to handle it gingerly; he had arranged earlier for it to be loaded with dummy cartridges.

Pijpekamp was straightening his jacket and flicking his trousers with the back of his hand. Pointing to Cor, the professor asked:

"Was it he?"

The young cadet, more piteous than ever, hardly looked like a criminal, simply like a guilty schoolboy. He hung his head and fidgeted, not knowing what to do with his hands.

They all went downstairs to the living room. Any came in last. Madame Popinga wouldn't sit down, and it was not difficult to guess that under her skirt her knees were trembling.

Now it was the inspector's turn to look embarrassed. He filled his pipe, lit it, then let it go out. He sat down in an armchair, but almost immediately jumped to his feet again.

"I've got myself mixed up in an affair that is no business of mine," he began jerkily. "A Frenchman came under suspicion, and I was sent to look into the matter. . . ."

To gain time he lit his pipe again. Then he turned toward Pijpekamp.

"Beetje is outside, and so is her father and Oosting. You'd better tell them to go home . . . or . . . or to come in here. . . . It all depends. Do you want the truth to come out?"

Without waiting to consider the question, Pijpekamp disappeared. A minute later Beetje entered shyly, then Oosting, frowning, and, last, Liewens, followed by Pijpekamp. The farmer was pale and nervous.

As soon as everybody was in the room, Maigret slipped out. They could hear him in the next room opening the sideboard. When he came back, he had a glass in one hand and a bottle of brandy in the other. Deeply gloomy, he drank alone. He seemed almost overawed by the presence of all these people.

"Well, Pijpekamp? Do you want the truth?"

When Pijpekamp didn't answer, he went on savagely:

"I don't suppose you do, and you may be right. But . . . never mind—it's too late now. Here it is, whether you want it or not. . . .

156

"You see, we belong to different countries, to different races . . . different climates too. . . . And as soon as you scented a family scandal you pounced on the first piece of evidence that would enable you to pigeonhole the case. A murder committed by some foreign sailor. . . . Perhaps you were right. Perhaps it would have been better that way. Better for public morals, better for the preservation of that good example the upper classes are supposed to set the people. . . . But I, on the other hand, I couldn't help thinking of Popinga. I couldn't help seeing him here in this room, playing with the radio, and dancing—dancing under the murderer's eye. . . ."

Maigret sighed. He looked at nobody as he went on:

"The revolver was found in the bathroom. So there was never any serious doubt that the shot came from inside the house. It would be ridiculous to think that the murderer, before running off, would have had the presence of mind and the coolness of judgment to throw it in through the window, which was open only a few inches . . . And also having previously burgled the house to put a cap in the bathtub and a cigar butt in the dining room."

He started walking up and down the room, still avoiding the eyes of his audience. Liewens and the Baes, who could not understand his words, stared at him intently, trying to divine their sense.

"That cap, the cigar butt, and, especially, the revolver taken from Popinga's desk—it was too much. . . . Do you see what I mean? . . . Somebody was overdoing it. Dragging too many red herrings across the trail. Oosting or someone else coming from outside might have left any one of those clues, two at the most, but certainly not all.

"We can proceed by elimination. . . . The first to drop out is the Baes. Are we really to suppose that he first went into the dining room to throw a cigar butt on the floor, then upstairs to look for Popinga's revolver, finally to leave his own cap in the bathtub? And all this without anybody seeing him?

"Next we can rule out Beetje. She never went upstairs during the evening, and thus could not have put the cap in the bathtub. Nor could she have taken the cap in the first place, since she was walking by Popinga's side.

"Her father could have killed Popinga, after seeing him with Beetje, in a sudden access of rage. But how could he have entered the house unnoticed?

"That leaves only Cornélius, apart from the household. He didn't go upstairs either, and if he'd pinched the cap, wouldn't Any have seen him? . . . He might have been jealous of his teacher, but—well, you've only to look at the boy! Does he look like he could commit a murder and not confess it within twenty-four hours?"

Maigret paused, knocking out his pipe against his heel, oblivious of the carpet.

"That's about all as regards outsiders. We are left with Madame Popinga, Any, and Jean Duclos. What proof is there against any one of them? Duclos came out of the bathroom with the revolver in his hand. Many would say that that proved his innocence. But it might also be a very cunning move. . . . There remains the question of the cap. Neither he nor Madame Popinga could have taken it without the other's complicity.

158

"As we've seen tonight, there's only one person who could have taken the cap. Any was left for a moment just as she was abreast of Oosting's boat.

"As for the cigar, there's no need to go into that. Here in Holland you can pick up an old cigar butt at any time of the day. . . . As regards leaving it in the dining room, Any was apparently the only one to enter that room during the evening. . . .

"But at the time the shot was fired she had about as good an alibi as it's possible to have."

Still shunning the gaze of his audience, Maigret laid some plans on the table, the plans Duclos had made of the house.

"It was impossible for Any to reach the bathroom without passing through her sister's room or the professor's. A quarter of an hour before the murder, she was known to be in her room, and no one saw her leave it, though both the other rooms were occupied. How, then, could she have fired a shot from the bathroom window?

"Any's been through legal training, and she's read books on criminology. She knows the value of material evidence. . . ."

The girl stood taut and rigid. She was obviously under great strain, but she did not lose her self-possession.

"To leave the crime for a moment, I must say something about Popinga. I'm the only person here who has never seen him, but I've managed to form a pretty clear idea of the man he was. . . . If he was thirsty for the pleasures of life, he was nonetheless easily intimidated by social conventions and established rules of conduct. In a reckless moment he made a pass at Beetje, but their subsequent relationship was as much her doing as his—if not much more. With the maid, he didn't go so far, because he didn't receive any great encouragement.

"A weakness for the fair sex—could one really call it more than that? He commits little peccadillos. He steals a kiss here and a kiss there. Sometimes more than a kiss.

"He has known life on the high seas and in foreign ports. An unfettered existence. But he is now in a permanent situation and a servant of the state, and he holds on to his post, to his house, to his wife. He's not in the least anxious to put his head in a noose. . . .

"He's torn both ways, and he strikes a compromise, the balance being heavily on the side of caution. . . .

"That's what Beetje never understood. Caution doesn't mean very much at the age of eighteen, and she thought he'd throw up everything to run away with her. . . .

"As Madame Popinga's sister, Any is soon on terms of easy familiarity with Conrad. She comes, so to speak, within his orbit. If she hasn't Beetje's looks, she is— well, she's a woman. I daresay Popinga had never met anyone like her before. She may have aroused his curiosity—a new line! Or perhaps it began only in playfulness. It may have tickled him to think of stealing Any from her precious books! Anyhow . . ."

The voice plodded on through the painful silence.

"I don't say she was his mistress, but with her, too, he had been, shall we say, imprudent. Sufficiently, anyhow, for her to have been taken in. She fell in love with him, though she was never altogether blind, like her sister, to the fact that he was a philanderer. . . .

160

"They were living in this house, a man and two women, Madame Popinga, blind, serene, and confident; Any, shrewd, passionate, and jealous. . . . It didn't take *her* long to realize that Conrad was carrying on with Beetje. Perhaps she'd looked for letters. Perhaps she'd found them. . . . She felt no resentment of her sister. The latter was Conrad's wife, and she was prepared to accept that. But with Beetje it was different. She couldn't admit Beetje's right to Conrad's affections. She couldn't bear the thought that those two might one day go off together.

"Rather than that . . . Yes, rather than that, wouldn't it be better to kill him?"

After a moment Maigret began again:

"That's all. Love turned to hate. At least, that's the simple formula for something that's no doubt very complex. . . . She began to play with the idea of killing him. She began to wonder how she could do so without leaving the smallest clue that could point in her direction. . . .

"And that very evening the professor talked of unpunished crimes and scientific murder! . . .

"Though passionate, she is nonetheless exceedingly proud of her intelligence. And she certainly is intelligent. She planned it very well. . . .

"She decided on a cigar butt as a means of throwing suspicion on an outsider. The alibi was carefully planned. She knew Conrad would see Beetje home, and knew that a hint would suffice to pin her sister to the window, watching anxiously for them to pass the lighted patch. . . .

"The cap was an afterthought, and, as I said before, it was just one thing too many. It spoiled the picture.

161

But, seeing it lying there on Oosting's boat, she was suddenly tempted to add a final clue. Getting rid of Cor for a second, she snatched it up.

"Even then, she was perhaps only toying with the idea of murder, getting a vindictive satisfaction out of the idea that she *could* kill him, that he was in her power. . . . But wasn't the whole evening conspiring to drive her forward?

"Conrad and Beetje holding hands during the lecture. Conrad and Beetje laughing, talking, dancing together. Conrad and Beetje riding off together. Always Conrad and Beetje! . . .

"Everything drifted on according to plan. The two rode off together. Madame Popinga and the professor were in their rooms. The hint was dropped, and Madame Popinga was peering out into the darkness, her heart standing still. . . .

"Then Any slips by in her underwear. . . . She has only to wait in the bathroom until Conrad comes around to the back with his bicycle. She waits. She shoots. She jumps into the bathtub and pulls down the lid. . . .

"Duclos dashes in, picks up the revolver, then runs downstairs, meeting Madame Popinga on the way. And when Any joins them in her underwear, isn't it obvious that she has rushed straight out of her room? In her underwear! Don't forget that. For her prudery has always been proverbial."

Drearily Maigret went on with the story:

"Only Oosting knew. He was standing in the cabin of his boat, looking through one of the portholes at the people going by. He saw Any take the cap. . . .

162

"He was Conrad's friend. Wouldn't he be the first to avenge him? Not at all! Respect for his dead friend, respect for the name Popinga—no scandal must be allowed to come near either. Not only did he hold his tongue, but he also prompted Cor to make a false statement to the police, designed to throw the blame on some foreign sailor.

"As for the others, they all suspected different people. Liewens, for instance, after seeing his daughter's letters, began to suspect her. Thinking I was going to arrest her, he tried to shoot himself.

"For her part, Beetje suspected her father, who didn't return home until after the crime, and who had perhaps discovered Conrad's relationship with her and inflicted a father's vengeance.

"Lastly, Cor, having seen Madame Popinga peering out the window toward the lumberyard, suspected her."

Maigret sighed. He still had a few more things to say.

"Now for tonight . . . When I made Any take the cap, no one thought much about it. Her cast-iron alibi had once and for all removed her from the list of suspects. But Any herself—surely she must now have known that I knew. That's what I wanted. That's why I made her take it. . . .

"We were reconstructing the crime. I was playing Popinga's part—I had openly announced it. Everybody was to do exactly what they had done before. If everybody did, wouldn't that give her her chance? In front of all, I told the professor to put the revolver on the bathroom windowsill.

"Why not get rid of me—the only person who could give her away? I'd be passing under the bathroom window, to put the bicycle away. The only question was whether the revolver would be loaded. But if it wasn't, she had only to leave it where it was.

"My plan miscarried. Madame Popinga didn't go to the window. . . .

"And someone else took Any's place. . . .

"That's the one redeeming act in this sorry story. The chivalry of the boy who wanted to save the woman he suspected, the woman who'd been like a mother to him. He's eighteen. One has to be eighteen to do things like that."

Again Maigret sighed.

"Yes, my plan miscarried. Without it, is there really any evidence against Any? I don't know. Nor do I care.

"It's in your hands now, Pijpekamp. I've told you the truth. Do what you like about it."

The Dutch detective moved reluctantly toward Any. The hollows under the girl's eyes devoured half her face, but she managed to say firmly:

"I'll answer any questions in the presence of my lawyer."

Maigret turned and walked slowly out of the room, followed by a calm but reproachful look from Oosting. As he left the house, he heard a flustered voice:

"A doctor . . . Quick!"

Madame Popinga, no doubt, with a heart attack . . .

Early next morning Maigret took the 5:05 from the little station at Delfzijl. He was alone. Nobody had thanked him. Nobody had come to see him off. Duclos had even deferred his departure till the next train, to avoid traveling with him.

The day broke as they came to a bridge over a canal. Boats were waiting with their sails slack. A man in uniform stood watching the train pass. As soon as it was over, he would turn the bridge on its pivot, and the traffic on the canal would resume.

Nearly three years later Maigret came across Beetje in Paris, where she was living with her husband, who was a salesman for light bulbs of Dutch manufacture. She had grown stouter.

Though she blushed at the sight of the inspector, she was soon talking about herself and her two children. Maigret gathered their situation, though comfortable, was by no means brilliant.

"And Any?" he asked.

"Didn't you hear about it? The papers were full of it. She killed herself with a fork only a few minutes before she was due to appear in court."

And Beetje added:

"You'll come and see us, won't you? . . . Avenue Victor Hugo, Number 28. . . . Only don't leave it too long, or you won't find us. We're going to Switzerland for a week of winter sports."

That day, at the Police Judiciaire, Maigret's subordinates found him unbearable.